TOO FAST FOR LOVE

Opportunistic Encounters

T0317991

mischief

This novel is entirely a work of fiction.
The names, characters and incidents portrayed in it are
the work of the author's imagination. Any resemblance to
actual persons, living or dead, events or localities is
entirely coincidental.

Mischief
An imprint of HarperCollins*Publishers*
77–85 Fulham Palace Road,
Hammersmith, London W6 8JB

www.mischiefbooks.com

A Paperback Original 2013

First published in Great Britain in ebook format by
HarperCollins*Publishers* 2012

Find out more about HarperCollins and the environment at
www.harpercollins.co.uk/green

Contents

Flaunting It
Rachel Kramer Bussel

When I reveal that my husband Brent and I have been together for half our lives, people are usually surprised, whether they're middle-aged like us, younger or older. At first, I bristled at their looks, as if there were something wrong with being a long-term couple, but, over the years, I've softened, become used to those responses. I understand them, as best I can. We aren't living in a time when couples tend to stick it out, and certainly not where they're still as passionate as they were when they first got together, or, in our case, more passionate. Their shock is indicative of what modern marriage has become, something fleeting, something to start with and move on to another arrangement later if things don't work out. Marriage isn't seen as a grand commitment but a grand adventure, and I'm living proof that a true sexual and soulful union can be both. Certainly, it hasn't been as easy as I'd thought it would be the day I walked down our makeshift aisle in the backyard of my friend Caroline's house, the Northern California sun glinting down on us, me in my mother's worn but beautiful dress, Brent in a tux that somehow looked too big on him, his stubbled face as handsome as I've ever seen it.

But our marriage is not intact simply because we took those vows way back in the mid-80s. It's intact because we've worked to keep it that way, to infuse even the darkest times with the fire that made us sleep together that very first night we met at a bar not too far off campus in Berkeley. My friends were delighted that I'd finally lost my virginity at twenty-three, and so was I, but, whereas they thought Brent was but a stepping stone to a college career of campus hookups, somehow I knew he was the real thing.

I wasn't his first – we're less than a year apart, but he was an early bloomer – but he's told me since that he feels in many ways like I was. I know I was the first woman he wanted to spend the night with, truly sleeping next to me, often worn out from our very vigorous sessions, in bed, on the floor, anywhere and everywhere, rather than keeping one eye on the clock until it was time to go. I was the first woman he fucked with the lights on, taking the time to look at every inch of me, even when I winced in half-delight, half-fear, urging him to enjoy the comforts of the dark. We couldn't keep our hands

2

off each other, but that doesn't mean we spent all day in bed; we were both active in campus groups, and we'd go hiking, do touristy things like walk across the Golden Gate Bridge, and argue our way back to his apartment after taking in the latest show at Berkeley Rep.

He became a professor, while I stuck around after getting a not-so-useful master's degree in sociology and went to school to become a therapist, consulting out of our home while raising our two kids. We were, and are, devoted parents, but we've always made sure to carve out time for us, where our undivided attention is on each other. Well, make that our almost undivided attention, because our real secret for staying together for over twenty years is that, when jealousy strikes, we don't ignore it, we address it directly, head-on. We examine it, celebrate it, flaunt it, and we've managed to turn it into a form of foreplay. Whereas some women get their claws out when another woman hits on their man, I curve my lips into a smile. Brent takes it one step further: he actively enjoys watching men hit on me, so much so that, if we're out with a group of friends and he notices a man checking me out, he'll comment on it, taking pride in my ability to attract barely legal freshmen all the way up to men with white hair. 'You can be a MILF *or* a sugar baby. I love that,' he told me once.

It took me a bit longer to get used to the girls who fawned over him, who would gladly have given new meaning to 'office hours', and not just for extra credit. I was proud that he still looked as sexy as he had in our student days, with an added gloss of maturity. He'd always been big, stocky, the kind of man who, feminist sensibilities be damned, I knew would protect me, so he didn't have to worry as much as some of his formerly thin friends about packing on the pounds. We tend to eat a healthy diet, marked with the occasional indulgence. The sweet young things didn't bother as much when I was closer to their age; now that they're younger than our kids, who've by now graduated college and settled on the East Coast, it can unnerve me a bit, but Brent makes sure I know he's always more amused than aroused.

'What would I even do with one of them, Nadine? I bet she barely knows what her G-spot is,' he'll whisper to me. 'Unless you wanted to help her find it.' And then we'll be off on a filthy fantasy in which we tag-team some innocent girl who we know deep down desperately wants it. That fantasy has come true a few times, once they've moved on to other professors for their formal classes, but what works best for us is the other way around; Bill is far more the voyeur than I am, and we've done everything from making our own sex tapes to screwing in front of windows where the chances of being seen are high.

Recently, though, while celebrating our twenty-seventh anniversary in Las Vegas (we celebrate every year, rather than simply waiting for the 'big' anniversaries), we took

4

our predilection for perversity to a new level. Aside from those women we'd bedded together, and a few steamy kisses at parties, I'd never been with anyone other than Brent, and definitely not another man. Oh, I'd looked plenty, online and off, and had my share of fantasies, but, up until then, simply telling Brent about my naughtiest daydreams had been enough. That was my way of flaunting it, and whenever my friends would tell me in hushed tones about lusting after their co-worker, lawn guy, painter or plumber, I'd wow them with stories of brazenly flirting right in front of my husband, and how hard it made him. The logical extension of these flirtations was something I'd been nervous about, always balking at actually taking things to the next level, but something about turning fifty had made me just a little bit bolder. I knew I looked good for my age, could pass for ten years younger if I wanted to, even though I'd let the grey overtake the brown.

Maybe it took that milestone to make me want to see what it was actually like to take another man to bed. The mere thought of it made me giddy with a kind of desire I hadn't felt since my earliest dates with Brent. We decided that we'd try it out and, if I met a man who tickled my fancy, I could go as far as I desired, as long as Brent could watch. I donned a black silk dress that was in stark contrast to the jeans and T-shirts on the crowd in the casino at The Flamingo, where we were staying. We'd chosen the Mandarin Oriental, since it didn't have a casino, as the debut of the new me, and booked a room there in hopes of using it as a home away from home, as it were. Taking another man back to the bed where I'd been intimate with Brent would be a bit much, even for me. I wanted a clean slate for what felt like losing a different kind of virginity. It took us a while to get out the door after our room-service meal, though, because Brent was so obviously, achingly hard, I had trouble keeping my hands, not to mention my mouth, off of him. By the time I'd given him an extremely agile blowjob, followed by him returning the favour as I sat on his face, my hair was mussed enough to require another brushing.

Finally, we were out the door. We held hands on our way down the strip, pausing to admire the Bellagio fountain, oohing and aahing as it erupted in front of a crowd of eager viewers, reminding me of Brent's cock when I jerked him off with my hand and I got to watch it spurt. Now *that* was a sight to behold. Then I stayed behind for ten additional minutes while Brent made his way to the bar and set himself up in a seat where he could easily watch the band – and the bar, which I sidled up to, making sure the slit in my dress was draped dramatically. I could feel men – and women – watching me, but the eyes that burned the brightest, the ones that made me blush, were Brent's. I just know when he's looking at me, whether from near or far, and, while I couldn't look back at him, I hoped he could feel me reacting to his gaze.

I smiled seductively at the bartender; there's nothing like making a man young enough to be my child blush, and really all it takes is slightly raised eyebrows, my favourite deep-red lipstick and my lips turned upwards into a smile that hints at all the magical things I can do with my mouth. 'What can I get you?' the man asked, his voice a little hesitant. I hoped I looked like I could eat him for lunch – or dessert, as it were.

'Veuve Clicquot,' I murmured, and no sooner had I turned around than another equally charming young man was asking if the seat next to me was taken. It was the seat closest to Brent, though, and I didn't want his view blocked.

'Not yet,' I said, giving him that same grin, one I'd had to practise when Brent and I first started flirting with others. I'd fallen into a married-lady smile, a benevolent 'look but don't touch' curve of my lips with other men and a 'you know I'm a sure thing' smile with Brent, but not the smile that promised a frisson of back-and-forth flirtation, a smile that said we could end up in Paris or naked on a rooftop. That was the smile I gave the stranger as I shifted casually, claiming the seat as if it had already been mine, making sure Brent had a perfect view of my back – my dress had a plunge in front and behind – and the young yummy stranger had a view of my cleavage.

'Are you even old enough to drink?' I teased him, running a sharp red nail, one I'd perfected over the last few weeks in lieu of my usual understated short pale-pink ones, along his arm.

'I'm twenty-three,' he said, thankfully holding off on adding 'ma'am', which would've added a little too much verisimilitude, then waited patiently, as if to see if he passed muster. When the bartender smiled at me, I said, 'And one for the gentleman,' not letting him order lest his preferred drink be something vile that would prevent me from lusting after him. I was here on a mission to bring home a memory that Brent and I could feast on for years to come, and I wasn't going to leave Vegas without completing it. But more than that, once I stopped playing the role of MILF ready to pounce on her prey and simply sat back and observed the young man, whose name was Andre, I felt confident, assured, grateful for every experience that had led me to this moment. When I was Andre's age, I'd never had the guts or even the desire to bed a stranger. Now, with my beloved husband watching, I knew I could do anything.

Once I realised I was completely in control of what might happen, that Andre was taking his cues from me – and so, for that matter, was Brent – I let go of any ideas of who I was or who I should be. I was me, of course, but a heightened, special, vacation-vixen version of me, and I was also someone whom Andre didn't know at all. He didn't need to know all of me – I was saving that, had always saved that, for Brent – but Andre could know this brand of me very, very intimately.

We sat and sipped our champagne, chatting lightly, each of us clearly plotting how to get the other one alone. Every time his arm brushed against me, or his eyes met mine, I willed myself not to blush like a schoolgirl. It was instinctual, after so long finding myself under Brent's steady, gorgeous gaze. I may be brazen in my fantasies, but in real life my pale skin reveals my giddiness, my nervousness, my excitement, and this moment had the added thrill of being watched twice, up close and from afar, by Andre and Brent. Every time I even thought about Brent seeing me with this young stud, I got wet and warm.

'I'm glad you have the night off,' I murmured, putting my empty glass down and leaning close enough so my breasts brushed against him. Not that it mattered since I'd already decided I wanted him, but Andre was a pianist, working parties and a few regular bar gigs. He'd dropped by to see a friend's band and stuck around. He'd bought my story about being in town for a conference.

Just as he put his glass down and reached for my hip, Brent got up and angled his way towards the bar. 'Excuse me,' he said as he jostled us. I thought I might come right there on the spot, with my boy-toy on my left, my husband on my right. Brent managed to convey all that he needed to in one lightning-quick, red-hot glance. I wanted to kiss him, then turn and kiss Andre, and, if I'd thought Andre would've gone for a little triple-play action, at that moment I'd have gone for it. Our little naughty experiment had turned me into a wild woman!

Instead, I let Brent order his scotch while Andre's hand roamed. When we took a break, I headed towards the bathroom, where I found a text from Brent. 'Go for it, baby,' it said. 'Take him back to the room and let me know when you're done. I wish I could be there to watch, but I'll be more than happy to hear about it.' Just reading the words made me wet, my mind racing with possibilities as the hairs on my arms stood on end.

Oh my God. I wanted to ask if he was sure, I wanted to pause and analyse whether this was a positive step in our relationship. OK, that's not exactly true; the rational, logical, organised side of me wanted to do that; the rest of me shivered in excitement, knowing I was about to taste and feel and touch a new man. That Brent wasn't just OK with what I was doing but seemed as eager as I was made me have even deeper respect for him.

I hurried back to Andre and settled myself flush against him. 'Well, well, well,' he said, smiling at me with those beautiful lips before using them to kiss the side of my neck, tenderly at first, then with a bit of tongue, followed by a light nipping of his teeth. I moaned softly, aware that we were probably the only people engaging in a public display of affection at the bar. 'Nadine,' he said, his voice husky and sweet. 'You are so beautiful.' I didn't hear a hint of 'so beautiful for your age' or 'so beautiful because I want to fuck you' in his voice. All I heard were those four words, and they in turn were beautiful to me.

This man, who could likely go home with any number of women in the room, taken or not, wanted me. 'I want you,' I heard him whisper, and I raised his face up to meet mine, staring into it a moment more, before reaching into my purse, pulling out enough for the bill plus a twenty-dollar tip, dropping it on the bar and pulling Andre towards the door.

'You've got me,' I said, leading him to the elevator. I didn't tell him I was married, not wanting to ruin a hint of the magic I could sense sparkling between us. That would be too real, and he didn't need to know; my marriage was mine and Brent's, and so was this encounter, in its way. I didn't want to explain what an older woman like me was doing waiting to be picked up at an elegant Las Vegas hotel, I just wanted to feel him next to me, on top of me, inside me. We slipped into the pristine hotel room, and I shuddered when I thought about the fact that Brent had the other key card and, if he wanted, could interrupt us at any time. He wouldn't, of course, but the possibility made me wet.

No sooner had we entered the room than Andre had pinned me to the door, his body pressed against me, young and hard and firm. He reached under my dress and felt me through my thin, now wet panties. An image flashed into my mind of him doing this in a back alley, to

11

a girl less than half my age, and that thought made me shudder. I wouldn't want to think about Brent with a girl half our age, but with Andre it was safe – and hot. 'You like that?' he asked, even though it was clear that I more than liked it. 'Turn around,' he said, easing up enough to let me mash myself against the door. 'Hold this up,' he said, lifting my long dress and pressing its hem into my hands. We had a huge suite at our disposal, yet he wanted me like this, pressed against the door, open and ready and wet as could be. Women my age didn't act like this – well, maybe they did, but I didn't, not really.

'Your ass is even hotter than it looked when you crossed the room, Nadine,' Andre murmured, then let his tongue detour down my spine as he easily slid my panties over my hips. Soon his lips were kissing my ass, his tongue sliding along my crack, teasing my opening while his fingers dove into my wetness. He pressed both inside me at once, those long, slender, beautiful young fingers – I wasn't sure how many – and his tongue, into my hole, somewhere even Brent had never placed his tongue. I pressed backwards against him, the sensations too glorious to not want more of them. He was bending his fingers in some way that made them seem even bigger, filling me as I pressed my ass against his face. I felt like I was dripping down the door, and it wasn't long before I couldn't stand up. I wanted to move to the bed, but Andre didn't seem in any rush.

He eased himself out of me and guided me so my body formed a V, like some naughty yoga pose, one I was grateful I could perform, with my hands flat on the lush carpet and my feet digging into the softness as well. Andre's fingers stroked my wetness again, this time just the outer edges of my pussy lips, before he smacked my ass, first one cheek, then the other. Each smack made me wonder how long I could hold the position, until his hand started lightly hitting my sex, my wetness. I whimpered in a totally unladylike way, but I was way beyond ladylike. He reached beneath me and circled my clit with his thumb and kept spanking me all over – my inner thighs, my cheeks, my pussy lips – until I was ready to beg for his cock, but Andre beat me to it.

When I was trembling so much I almost couldn't stand, he stood and guided me up, then lifted me and threw me onto the bed. When I landed I ached for his cock. I had already almost forgotten this was about me and Brent sharing an adventure, because Andre had transported me somewhere even more exciting. I wasn't just a married woman looking for a fling but, for a little while, a woman who'd do anything for this hot stud's cock, and he knew it. 'See something you want?' he asked as his eyes followed mine to the bulge in his trousers.

'Yes,' I managed, but, before I could say more, he'd taken out a cock that was even more impressive than anything I could've pictured. Don't get me wrong, I love

13

my husband's cock, I love every part of him, but Andre's was like a work of art, thick and wide and tall and proud. I reached for it, but he pushed my hand back.

'I don't want my cock in your hand. I want it in your mouth, and then your ass, and, if you're good, your pussy.' I whimpered again, then scrambled around so I could swallow it. I did, in one smooth thrust, but Andre intercepted me again. 'Not so fast, greedy girl. If you take my cock all the way down your throat like that, I'm gonna come, and I don't want that to happen just yet. Go slow. Focus on the tip. I'll fill your pretty mouth up later.' His words made me ache all over, my nipples stiffening, my pussy getting tighter, my ass clenching with want as I looked up at him while I ran my tongue around that hot, glorious swollen flesh. He smiled at me, and I moaned, reaching down to play with my clit, wondering if he'd object.

I shut my eyes and focused on the pure joy of pleasing this man who was young enough to be my son, who was hot enough to have his pick of women. If only Brent could see me now; that thought made me groan, and my open mouth led to Andre's dick sliding deeper down my throat, far enough that I might have gagged if I wasn't so in tune with our actions. I scrambled to go back to just sucking the tip, but he dragged me up by my hair. 'Get on the floor, on your knees, and put your hands behind your back,' he ordered. I was kneeling in seconds, my breasts pressing forward, arching towards him, my bare feet resting against my ass as he slapped his cock across my face. 'Don't worry, I know your ass is ready for me, ready to take all of this. Isn't it, Nadine?'

I replied as best as I could in my position and kept on sucking, until I had to gasp when his fingers reached for my nipples and pinched hard.

'Keep going, slut,' he said, and I did, tears of joy and arousal rushing to my eyes. I wanted to be his slut, his hot young ready-for-anything slut. I gagged on his cock, my saliva dripping from my mouth, as he took his pleasure from me before easing me up then pulling me towards his lips for a wet, hot kiss. 'I hope you have some lube,' he said, ''cause I'm going to fuck your ass even if you don't.'

Just having him mention lube let me know he wouldn't do anything that would truly hurt me; we'd chosen our hotel knowing they had a sex kit available for purchase, and I nodded and inclined my head towards the corner of the room.

Andre pushed me backwards and told me to get on all fours with my ass in the air. I heard my phone beep with a text message, Brent's special signal, and moaned, wondering what he would think if I didn't respond. Then Andre took matters into his own hands, wandering towards my phone. He picked it up, and silently read through my texts. 'Who's Brent?' he asked.

'My husband,' I said, my cheeks heating worse than they had when he'd slapped his cock against them.

'He wants to know what we're doing. Should I tell him I'm about to fuck you in the ass?'

Oh my God. Any answer I gave would be shameful – and arousing. If I answered Brent honestly, I'd be letting him know that I wasn't all his, not now, not ever. If I let Andre respond, I was telling my husband that another man had read his messages, had taken over for a little while. Either way, Andre now knew exactly what I was up to.

'Yes, tell him, and say I'll call him when we're done.' I buried my head in the pillows like a schoolgirl, my pussy clenching as I wondered whether that text would make Brent hard – or mad. Either way, he'd surely fuck me later and let me know. Andre texted back, the fingers that had been buried inside me now flying fast and furious against the screen of my phone. It only took a minute at most, but it was an agonising minute as I waited, my ass in the air, hungry for him.

Soon he was back on the bed, those same fingers finding their way to my clit, rubbing my wetness until I wanted to push back against him, force him inside me, but I didn't, because that was an illusion; Andre was in charge, and he wanted my ass. 'Hold your cheeks open for me, Nadine, while I put on a condom,' he said.

If I'd thought having Andre text Brent was humiliating,

holding my cheeks open for him was even more so. I was grateful my head was buried in the clean, crisp sheets, my now messy hair hiding my blush as I waited for him to enter me. First he poured several drops of lube along my crack, then rubbed them in with the head of his cock. Then Andre was entering me, slowly, carefully, as only a man who's fucked a woman's ass before can. I pictured the same girl I'd seen in my mind earlier, the one in the back alley, taking him into her ass. I pictured Brent fucking me while we watched them, and soon my backdoor muscles were drawing him deeper into me.

'Oh, God, yeah,' he said, easing slowly back and forth.

Andre lost his cool, dom, collected demeanour after his cock plunged all the way into my ass. 'You're so fucking tight, Nadine, I bet your husband doesn't fuck your ass often enough, does he?'

I'd have been disloyal if I'd answered the question, so I just moaned, because it was true and not true; Brent fucked my ass plenty, but, with Andre's dick inside me, it definitely didn't feel like I was getting my proper share of buggering.

Soon his words melted into nonsense, his full length seamlessly working its way in and out of me. 'I'm not going to get to fuck your pussy, Nadine; he'll have to do that, because I'm gonna come very soon,' Andre said, leaning down and biting the back of my neck, surely hard enough to leave a mark.

17

I squirmed and bucked back towards him, then shuddered when he reached for my clit. His tongue and teeth on my neck, his cock inside me, his gorgeous fingers on my most tender part, were too much. I screamed into the sheet, my orgasm taking over, and moments later I felt him explode inside me. The pulse of his seed seemed to go on for minutes.

Andre eased out and lay next to me, panting. My phone beeped again and he reached for it, then handed it to me.

'Having fun?' Brent asked. The phone beeped again while I held it, with an incoming photo of Brent's cock, hard and firm, making me smile.

'Yes, baby,' I typed. 'But come back soon; it's never truly fun without you.'

I knew Andre was watching over my shoulder, and I didn't care. He knew my secret, and he wasn't put off by it. We'd enjoyed each other and that was more than enough; sure, if I were single, I'd have gladly spent the night with him, but I didn't feel like I was missing out. I never did, not with Brent, my Brent, ready to join me.

Andre proved to be an old soul. I'm sure plenty of guys his age would have been offended, would have taken my text as an insult. He simply got up, washed himself off, then put his clothes on. 'I'd give you my number, but it sounds like you don't need it,' he said, then gave me a kiss that took my breath away. We both heard the key card in the door just as Andre put on his jacket, and my two lovers for the evening passed in the night without so much as a word.

Brent climbed into bed and kissed the same spot on my neck where Andre's lips had been only twenty minutes before. 'Tell me everything,' he said, and, as he lifted my hips and entered me, I did.

Tea Dresses
Sommer Marsden

The bell made me look up. I put my chopsticks in my soup bowl and straightened up to try and peek. It was hard to see a clear way from the counter to the front door with all the stock I'd just bought.

Maybe it was best I didn't see him coming. The look of him slammed me like a fist wrapped in cotton.

'I'm looking for a dress.'

'You'd look much better in a vintage suit, if you don't mind me saying,' I teased.

I was shocked I got even that out. He was tall and broad and looked very much a thug from the 1920s. His dark hair so close-cut it almost looked like he was bald on first glance. He had dark-brown eyes – so fucking dark you couldn't distinguish the pupil from the iris – and they seemed to see right down into the bones and meat of me.

But he smiled and, when he twisted his mouth that way, something in me twisted.

Jesus.

'I think you're right. But the dress isn't for me. It's for this girl I'm seeing. For a party my boss's wife is throwing. A tea party.' He wrinkled his nose when he said it and I laughed.

My ears picked up two things. The way he said 'this girl' meant she wasn't a serious thing. He didn't say 'my girlfriend' or 'my fiancée' or 'the woman I'm dating'. It was way more casual than that, and that sent a shiver up my spine like a tiny piece of ice being dragged along my skin.

'I see. You sound very excited about this tea party.'

'I'd rather be dipped in shit. Or boiled in oil.' He stuck out his hand. 'Mack.'

'Gretchen. And I think I have just the thing. Believe it or not, today of all days, a woman brought in a whole case of clothes from her great-grandmother's attic. At least three of them are tea dresses.'

'No shit,' he said. He spoke like a thug too. But those eyes were intelligent and underneath the beleaguered I-am-annoyed gaze … soft. Kind.

I imagined his hands on me, I couldn't help it. And, when I let myself go there, a slick rush of fluid slipped free of me, staining my panties with my sudden and intense interest.

21

I sucked in a shuddery breath. 'No shit. Can I get them out for you?'

That's when he really stopped to look at me. His dark gaze dragging from my chocolate-coloured bob cut to my sweetheart-neckline sweater to my pencil skirt. And then back up again.

Heat and lust rushed colour to my cheeks and he didn't miss it. Not for a second. 'Yeah. Get them out for me, Gretch. If you will.'

He planted his meaty hands on my spotless glass counter. I'd just washed it. But I didn't mind. I was too busy trying to breathe without panting like a dog.

'Be right back.'

I hurried off. When had my shop gotten so close? So tiny? There didn't seem to be enough air in the place for me and Mack. But I would make do. I would have to.

I pulled the first dress from the garment bag. A butter-yellow frock with crinoline beneath the skirt. Low-cut without being slutty, floaty without being too much of a princess dress. I put my hair up ... down ... up and then down again. Letting it float around my face as I tried to steady my breathing.

'What the fuck,' I sighed and nixed the panties, leaving them in a heap on the floor in the corner of the dressing room. When I exited, I pushed my feet into taupe-coloured heels someone had brought in on consignment.

'All in,' I said and, as I passed the front door, I quietly

flipped the sign to CLOSED and locked the door by pressing the button on the knob.

I rounded the corner to find him lounging in my chair behind the counter like he owned the joint. The cocky nature of his demeanour made me squirm beneath the dress. I wanted him. There was no denying what my body was saying.

'Nice,' he grunted. And, as if Mack could read my thoughts or feel the lust coming off of me, he crooked a finger at me and said, 'Come here. Give us a close-up look.'

I stepped to him as if we'd done this a thousand times before instead of having just met. He ran a thick finger over the smooth embroidered skirt of the dress. I felt each stroke he left on the fabric as if he'd touched me. I licked my lips and waited.

'I like the cut. How it shows off your legs. Of course, your legs are better than hers.' With that, his hand cupped the back of my knee and I felt my legs go weak.

'Nice calves,' he went on, moving just a bit so his reach allowed him to run his cupped palm from the back of my knee down the hard muscle of my calves.

Inside me, odd things were happening. A tingling buzz had taken up residence in my tummy and my pussy constricted eagerly around nothing at all. But it was all too easy to picture it growing tight around his thrusting cock. I'd lay odds his cock was thick and sturdy like his fingers.

'But it's a tiny bit too short,' Mack grumbled. 'Because I can do this.' His hand surged up the back of my thigh, damn near buckling my legs, and found my right buttock. That hand felt as big as a catcher's mitt warmed in the sun.

I sighed and he gave me a crooked grin. Out of nowhere he pulled his hand free of my ass and then smacked it back down again, fast and hard. I jumped and my muscles went stiff with shock.

'You said there were more?'

I nodded, not trusting my voice or my perpetually thumping cunt at this point. If I moved, I thought I might come. I waited.

'I want to see another one. That OK with you?'

His hand was once again resting nonchalantly on my calf and my muscles tingled and twitched. Only his thumb was moving in restless little sweeps along my skin. I nodded.

'Then let's see one. My favourite colour is green,' he said. 'Just an FYI.'

I hurried away, fearful my pussy was so wet I'd leave marks on the dress. Fearful that he could hear my heart. Fearful that he could smell my lust on the air. And entirely turned on.

I wrestled free of the butter-yellow dress and tossed it haphazardly on a wooden hanger. Then I found what I was looking for in the bag. A sea-foam-green frock with a square neckline and a lace hem.

I stepped into it, being careful not to snag the heel of my shoe on the stitching. And trying very hard not to fall over. That would totally not be sexy. I fluffed the skirt and twirled once in the mirror. My gut was currently in my throat and my pulse a wild untamed thing that made my head ache with its rhythm.

I pushed the curtain back and walked as slowly as I could. Forcing myself to breathe. Forcing myself to exude sex. Not that I really felt I needed to. There had been this lightning strike of attraction between us from the get-go. The sight of him in my chair only solidified it – legs splayed, hand resting on his fly where a very real, very obvious erection pushed against the black fabric of his trousers.

'I like it,' he said, motioning me forward. His hand found the back of my knee as if he'd touched me a million times before. My body responded as if he had.

I puffed out air softly, almost like I was trying to shout but had no voice, when he slid his hand high up the back of my leg, beneath the virginal floaty skirt of the tea dress. He cupped that tight muscle along the back of my thigh that got taut and sore when I ran too many times in a week. And then he was holding my ass cheek in his big hand, giving it tiny little squeezes that made my juices flow more aggressively.

'You have the ass of a thoroughbred,' he told me.

'Is that a compliment?'

He squeezed again and then his hand meandered around my hipbone to my front. He was suddenly – blissfully – palming my mound now. 'Does it feel like a compliment?'

'God, yes,' I wheezed.

Mack gave a single nod of his giant head and very nonchalantly parted my nether lips with his thick fingers. Instantly, he located the tight bud of my clitoris, now screaming with want and blood, and stroked me there. My knees shook, threatening to dump me on my ass, but I tightened my muscles and forced myself to breathe.

'You're slick. In green. Wet like the ocean. Green like sea water, green like grass. Wet and slick and all in green.' He chuckled out his nonsense sentences and then pushed a broad finger into me.

A bubble of laughter burst out of me. It felt good. Too good. And what was I doing? I had never done this before in my store. But then again, I'd never ever felt any on-the-spot lust close to this before. Not this consuming.

He fucked me with his broad fingers, never pulling those dark eyes away. 'Good?'

I could only nod. Steadying myself with one hand on his broad shoulder. Under the cloth he was warm and sturdy and I imagined I could feel his heartbeat, a wild current running up into my fingers and travelling up my arm.

'I have a pink one,' I managed. My tongue was too big for my mouth, my heartbeat too loud to hear above.

26

'Do you now?'

Another nod from me and Mack caught my wrist in his hand and pulled me so I bent over him. He peeked down the front of my modest square neckline and then pushed my hand over the hard ridge of his cock. He was long and thick and held at bay by nothing more than a pair of grey slacks and whatever he was sporting underneath.

His big hand crushed my much smaller one around his erection and he thrust up hard and fast – just enough to show me what it would be like were he thrusting into me.

'This girl –' I started, cocking an eyebrow at him. Forcing myself to meet his gaze.

'Is just a girl. Not a girlfriend, not a fiancée, not a wife. Just a girl. Now go put the other one on.'

I believed him and I hurried off on my taupe high heels, feeling like the devil was on my tail, prompting me to sin. I loved it.

The pink dress had a ruched bodice that cinched me up and showed off my tits. It gave the illusion of a wasp waist from the way it flared out. A very unsubtle sweep of cotton-candy-pink fabric. Along the hem on the left side was a series of small hearts stitched in silver thread. It was the only adornment. Which is why I liked the pink one the best, though I normally loathed pink.

But this pink made me think of lips and tongues, kisses and fucking, soft wet things and orgasms. Or that could just be the way my mind was working right about now.

'Are you coming?' He chuckled.

'Not yet, but soon,' I murmured under my breath.

I hurried out, the curtain of the dressing room billowing behind me. I passed the front door and watched a parade of people on their lunch break stroll past. One woman headed to my door and my heart skipped a beat, but then she caught sight of the CLOSED sign and kept going.

'Come on, cupcake,' Mack growled and the fine hairs on my neck rose and tingled.

'Coming,' I breathed and hurried on. With a grand flourish, I stepped behind the counter and curtseyed.

He had his cock out. In hand. It didn't even faze me. It seemed most logical, because we were going to fuck, after all. That was a no-brainer. Seeing him handling himself that way, stroking his hard-on with his huge hand, had a storm of emotions roiling in my gut. Excitement, fear, lust, want, anxiety. It was a heady mélange of feelings that left me breathless and weak-kneed.

'Come on,' he said.

So I went, forcing my stunned body to move towards him. I stood close enough that he barely had to reach out to touch me, and watched him – mesmerised by the motion of it – handle his cock.

'Kneel for me, Gretch,' he said, using his instantaneous nickname for me.

I dropped to my knees, licking my lips. Quite often my eager show of need to suck cock was simply a ploy to turn my partner on. Not now. Not this time. This time I truly wanted to suck his cock. Wanted to feel the hard velvety tip of him slide along my lips like I was applying gloss. I wanted to taste that first salty drop of pre-come and swirl my tongue around the impudent helmeted tip of him. I wanted it all so much that I was already leaning in to do all of that and more.

Mack moved back just a bit and laughed. 'Look at you. Just gagging for it. Hold on.'

Then he wrapped his hand in my hair, forming a tether, and yanked so my head went back and my eyes went to his. 'Just so we're on the same page. You're going to suck my cock.'

I tried to nod, forgetting his grip.

'And then I'm going to do whatever I want.'

Again I tried to nod. Short memory and all that. He smiled at me. The hard lines of his rugged face softening for a moment. When I smiled back, he pushed my head forwards steadily but not hard enough to hurt me.

My mouth came down, lipsticked and desperate on the soap-scented skin of his cock. I trailed my tongue over the small drop of fluid at the tip, collecting it. When I sucked the head of his erection into the heat of my mouth, he made a noise in his throat. Forcing myself as low as I could go, I ate him up inch by inch until my lips almost touched the base of his erection. His pubic hair tickling at my nose. This close to his skin he smelled like the ocean and cold air. It was a good smell and I inhaled greedily both to steady my beating heart and take the scent of him into myself.

'Good, good,' he said. Almost like he was talking to himself.

His hand in my hair allowed me to turn my head just enough so that I could sweep my open mouth up one side of his length and down the other, my open-mouthed kiss making his skin wet as I dragged my lips. I felt his fingers tighten in my hair, saw his muscles bunch as he tensed in my chair.

'Stand up, Gretch.'

But I chased him with my mouth instead, managing to snake my tongue out over him to taste him one more time. He gripped my hair tight and pulled my head back. With a short push, he moved me back and rose at the same time. Big hands curled to my dress-cinched waist and lifted me gently onto a short table behind the counter. It was where I folded clothing. The antique wooden table was small – the perfect size – taller than my chair but shorter than the glass counter. He dropped me there gently and pushed my fluffy skirt up around my waist, baring me to his gaze.

'Hold your skirt up, princess,' he said. And then he dropped back into my chair and rolled towards me, the casters sighing on the old linoleum floor.

His mouth was searing on my pussy lips, his tongue

intrusive in the best possible way. Insinuating itself into my wet folds, seeking out and finding my rigid clitoris. I gripped the lip of the table and held on tight. I didn't want to come so fast. Fuck. Not so fast.

He wasn't gentle or shy about it. He pressed his mouth, generous for such a hard-looking man, to the lips of my pussy and ate me in earnest. I gripped the wood beneath my fingers hard and held myself at bay. Barely. I wanted to grab him and hold his shoulders and thrust up rudely against his seeking tongue, but managed not to. I let him do what he wanted. Which was taste me – slow but not too slow, rough but not too rough – fan-fucking-tastic. I thought I'd gotten away with it, but at the last minute he pressed my thighs wide with his strong hands and sucked my clit hard, bit it gently and then thrust his tongue into my weeping cunt before sucking again.

I came with the sound you would get if a laugh and a sob had a baby. My body shook uncontrollably as the orgasm rolled through me, little pink sparkles to match my tea dress blooming in the darkness behind my closed eyelids. He held me firm with his hands on my thighs as it lessened somewhat.

'Don't move.' He stood, took his heavy cock in his hand and sidled up between my thighs. His legs pressed against the table, his button and zipper scraping at me a little as he stroked the head of his cock along the soaking wet split of me.

31

'Move forward some,' he finally commanded.

I did it. Lulled and mesmerised by his voice. The easy way he commanded without sounding like a jerk or a prick.

A single swift thrust brought him deep into me. My still tight pussy eating up his erection as he drove in hard. Big hands cupping my ass through the silly fluffery of my dress.

'Kiss me, kiss me,' I begged, finally speaking.

He did. My shoulder and then my neck so I shivered. Then my hair and my ear, before finally bringing his lips down on mine. His tongue tasting of my pussy. The musky sweet taste of my own sex and juices.

He hauled me forward roughly, grunting like a beast as he found a place inside of me that apparently pleased him very much. 'Good,' he said.

'Good,' I echoed, though I wasn't sure if it had been a question. I was pretty sure it wasn't.

Mack found my clit with his thumb and my pulse with his teeth. It wasn't hard for him to make me wetter that way. Or make me beg. His mouth was sharp and insistent as it scraped my skin. His breath rolling bursts of thunder in my ear. He pressed that tiny hard nub of flesh that made me shiver and said, 'Come on, Gretch, give it to me.'

No one was allowed to call me Gretch. I hated dirty talking – thought it was stupid.

Until now.

He pressed my clit again, rocking his hips just so until I felt the blissful tightening of internal muscles, the flood of heat, the apex of tension and then the blissful waterfall effect of a really strong orgasm.

'There she is.' He chuckled as I held his big biceps with my hands. My thighs trembled and my arms responded in kind.

'Here I am.' I pushed at him suddenly with my forearms. Shoving him back so he had to move.

His rough mug twisted into a smile. 'Are we going to be that way?'

'Yes ... I mean no!' I gasped. 'Let me up. Please,' I finished, 'I need –'

Someone knocked on the door and my eyes flew to the clock. Oh shit. My one o'clock consignment appointment had arrived. Our eyes met, his impossibly dark, mine frantic, I'm sure. He cocked an eyebrow, waiting.

'Ignore it,' I blurted and pushed him a bit harder. My feet hit the floor and my knees did a little wiggly dance that threatened to spill me on my ass. My body was still throwing off brilliant echoes of my orgasm and I could feel heat in my cheeks like fire.

'Where you going, Gretch?' he asked, pulling my bodice out from my breasts with his finger.

'Nowhere, here ...' I wasn't making any sense, so, when he shoved his big hand into the front of my fluffy pink frock and pinched my nipples so hard I almost came again, the moan I let out fit right into the conversation.

I wiggled away from him and turned my back to his mass. Heart beating so hard it was damn near all I could hear, I rucked up the back of my new dress, held it tight to my waist and bent over the antique wooden table he'd just fucked me on. I presented myself, legs apart so he could feel or see the wetness of my pussy should he choose to.

'Please,' was all I managed.

He dragged it out – cocky bad boy that he was – by sliding each finger along my drenched slit. He'd find my clit and press it or pinch it or just swirl a broad fingertip over it until I was damn near vibrating. Then he gave a grunt that told me he had reached the end of his amusement with this game. He came in close behind me, making the fine hairs along my skin hum and sway, and kicked my legs a bit further apart.

And then he was in, driving deep, filling me up and stretching me wide and gripping my bare hips in his strong hands the way that made me crazy.

'You like it from behind, do you?'

I could only nod.

When he rotated his hips from side to side a little, making tender places deep inside me flex and grasp at him, I saw tiny fairy lights in my vision. I was holding my breath, I realised, so I exhaled. It was a shuddering, desperate sound.

'Dirty, dirty, dirty.' He chuckled and then his rhythm caught fire. Mack drove into me hard and fast, inching my high-heel-sheathed feet off the ground until I was a faux ballerina, only my toes touching the linoleum, the wooden table shaking with his efforts and my violent motions.

'Yes,' I told him.

'Yes?'

I nodded, my hair swishing on the wood. I could hear his suit trousers whispering as he pounded into me. His thumb found the tight star of my anus and I froze before relaxing into the bite of pain and shoving back to force his hand. He slid into me further there, so the hint of pain amped up the rush of pleasure.

'Yes, yes,' I countered, laughing a little.

It made no sense. It made perfect sense.

'You're so dirty you're pushing me past my limit, Gretch.' There was humour in his voice, but something more.

Truth.

His thumb pushed deeper, his motions frantic. He wiggled his thumb in my bottom and rasped, 'Touch yourself.'

He didn't have to tell me twice. I got my arm under my body, thinking wildly how insane and inappropriate this all was. And how fucking perfect and exciting as well.

Rubbing my clit in greedy little bursts I felt him go rigid and, when he uttered, 'Fuck me hard,' I came. His orgasm nipping at the heels of mine as he thrust so hard

35

my pretty taupe shoes actually did leave the floor and we were both laughing.

'Wow … wow …' I stayed sprawled across the table. There was a tickly sensation as he ran his finger up the zipper of the dress and then stroked the bare skin of my back above the fabric.

'Wow is a good start.' Mack pulled free of me and backed up so I could right myself.

When I turned to him, the red in my cheeks was flagrant.

'So?' I cleared my throat. 'Do you like any of those options? The dresses?' I fluffed the pink skirt and shifted a little, every filthy thing we'd just done running through my head.

'I liked them all,' Mack growled, pulling me in gently by the delicate bodice. 'Have to admit, though, the pink was my favourite.'

I smiled. 'Mine too.'

'And you look really great in it.'

'Thanks.'

He kissed me, his tongue stroking mine for a minute. Then, 'I was thinking, maybe you'd like to go to a tea party.'

'But that girl –'

He grabbed my ass and kissed me again. 'She's just a girl.'

The Game's Afoot
Rose de Fer

'Jake? Aren't you going to get dressed?'

Lauren stood staring at her husband. He was slumped in front of the telly in baggy tracksuit bottoms and a T-shirt he'd had since the 80s.

'Break his bloody legs, the cheating bastard!' he shouted at the screen. 'Huh? What, babe? Aw shit, was that today?'

He looked up at her with an expression of dismay that might have matched her own. She could see the effort it had already cost him to tear his eyes away from the match, could sense his horror at the possibility that he might actually have to switch it off and go with her to visit her sister.

How should she play this? Insist and suffer his resentment all afternoon – and probably the rest of the week? Or let him off and pretend to be satisfied with the inevitable flowers and a promise of dinner at the weekend? Why did everything have to involve so much calculated manoeuvring? If she'd known married life would turn out to be an endless strategy game, she'd have stayed single.

'It's OK,' she said finally. 'Really. Maria and I can just –'

She hadn't even finished her sentence when Jake's attention was reclaimed by the TV.

'What? That was a fucking mile offside!'

Lauren sighed. 'Right, well, I'll see you later,' she said and turned to go. If he said goodbye to her, she missed it in the barrage of profanities that followed her out the door.

She didn't blame Jake for forgetting about the lunch date. Maria could be tiresome. All she wanted to talk about was her ongoing attempts to get pregnant and Lauren found herself secretly hoping it would never happen. She didn't get on with babies and didn't want to have to hurt her sister's feelings by refusing to play doting auntie if and when the time came.

After an interminable lunch, Lauren found herself resenting both her sister and her husband for spoiling her day.

She wasn't ready to go home and face Jake again. He'd either be grieving or celebrating and neither was likely to do anything for her mood. So she took herself to the mall, where she decided a little retail therapy would at least make her feel like the day hadn't been a total loss.

Her first stop was the bookstore, where she succumbed to the temptation of a three-for-one offer. She hadn't finished the novel she was currently reading and she already had a teetering to-be-read stack on her bedside table. But she wasn't going to let that stop her. How many computer games had Jake bought over the years that he'd never even played?

She tried on sexy shoes and dresses as she made her way through the shops, but her heart wasn't really in it. Where could she wear those four-inch leopard-print heels and clingy little black dress anyway? Dinner at the pub? There was certainly little danger of Jake taking her somewhere posh like the theatre. Or even out dancing.

The last time she'd gone comfort shopping she'd picked up a slinky black lace nightie, hoping it would spur Jake into action. If he would put even half the energy into sex that he put into berating referees and players on the telly she'd be a happy woman. But after making a few initial noises of appreciation, he'd merely gone through the motions of sex as if performing a duty and then fallen asleep immediately afterwards. Lauren had resigned herself to a lifelong affair with her vibrator.

What was the point? A pair of fuck-me shoes wasn't going to save her sex life. With a heavy heart, she dropped them back into their box and left the shop. As she made her way towards the mall's exit with only the books to show for her outing, she heard a voice behind her.

'Excuse me, miss!'

She turned along with several other women, but it was clearly Lauren who was being hailed.

'Yes?'

A willowy Japanese girl stood there, dressed in a vibrant purple silk blouse and a short, tight black skirt. She was strikingly beautiful, with long, glossy black hair and ivory skin. Lauren had never thought of herself as bi but there was something about the exotic beauty of Oriental women that had always appealed to her. And this girl was a vision.

She made a little bow and Lauren instinctively returned the gesture. The people around them continued on their way, probably disappointed that they weren't about to see a shoplifter apprehended.

'Sorry to chase you down like that,' the girl said, 'but I happened to notice you trying on those shoes.'

'Shoes?' Lauren echoed.

'Yes. The leopard ones.'

'Oh, those. Yes, well, they were a bit over the top. For my usual night out, I mean.'

The girl smiled, a little coyly. 'Actually, it wasn't the shoes that got my attention. It was your feet.' Her English was perfect, an odd and appealing counterpoint to her strong Japanese accent. There was no chance that something had got lost in translation or that Lauren had misunderstood her.

'My feet?' she asked.

'Yes. I'm from the salon over there.' The girl pointed. 'Beauty and Serenity. We're doing a special promotion, you see, and we need a pedicure model.' She raised her eyebrows expectantly.

Lauren shook her head in confusion. Was this some kind of prank? 'But if you saw me trying on the shoes, then you must have seen my feet. They look awful.'

'No,' the girl said with an insistent shake of her head. 'They're perfect! What we'd like to do is give you a pedicure and photograph the result for our ad campaign. We'd pay you as well, of course.'

Lauren could hardly believe this was happening. Her? A model? *Pay* her? She peered closely at the girl's face, searching for signs that she was about to burst into laughter or glance over at a hidden camera. But she looked completely sincere, her eyes wide and hopeful, her smile sweet and inviting.

'Well, I ...'

'Brilliant!' The girl beamed happily and took Lauren by the arm to lead her towards the salon. 'I'm Kumiko, by the way.'

Lauren introduced herself and went where she was led. Maybe the day was turning around after all.

The private room Kumiko took her to was more

elegant than the humble shopfront suggested. Flowers bloomed in little pots dotted around the room and soft music issued from hidden speakers. Kumiko guided her to a chair and placed a basin of water at her feet. A scattering of pink and white orchids floated on the surface.

Lauren kicked off her shoes and sighed with contentment as she eased her bare feet into the warm scented water and rested her hands on the arms of the chair. Kumiko knelt beside the basin and washed each foot with her soft and gentle hands, slipping her fingers in between Lauren's toes and massaging the delicate skin of her soles.

Although she wasn't ticklish, her feet were extremely sensitive and the focused attention was making the tiny hairs tingle all over her body. She noted with some surprise that it was the same kind of gooseflesh she got when she was sexually aroused. She shivered as Kumiko withdrew her feet from the water one at a time and patted them with a soft towel. When they were dry, she moved the basin aside and smiled up at Lauren.

'I hope your husband appreciates such lovely feet,' she said slyly.

Lauren blushed, uncertain how to respond to the strange compliment. She'd never thought of any feet – especially her own – as lovely. You either pampered them to make them less ugly or you hid them with killer shoes.

'I'm afraid he's more interested in football than feet.'

'That's a shame,' Kumiko continued. She lifted Lauren's right foot and held it with all the care of a museum curator handling a priceless artefact. 'Look how high the arch is, how delicately formed the toes are. And the skin is so soft and smooth. You obviously take very good care of your feet.'

That was only true by default. Her feet were more often snuggled inside fluffy socks and comfy trainers than glamorous but punishing heels.

'And this –' Kumiko wiggled the longer second toe '– is so refined. It's what they call the Greek foot. Statues of Aphrodite have toes like yours.'

'Really? I always thought it was a bit ... freaky.'

'Oh no! I think it's the most beautiful type of foot there is.'

She left Lauren pondering that thought while she opened a little bottle of oil. Lauren caught the rich aroma of cherries. Kumiko drizzled the oil over the top of one foot and the heavenly scent seemed to intensify by the second.

'Nice, isn't it?' Kumiko said, noticing Lauren's reaction.

'Gorgeous.'

Lauren stared down at her feet as though seeing them through new eyes. Quite apart from pointing out any aesthetic qualities, Kumiko was also stimulating her in unusual and confusing ways. She leaned back in the chair as she felt the oil begin to warm against her skin.

43

Kumiko's fingers painted the oil across the top of Lauren's instep and down the length of each toe before sliding her thumbs underneath to press the sensitive arch beneath. The feeling was exquisitely sensual and Lauren couldn't restrain a little moan as Kumiko's thumbs skilfully erased every bit of tension.

When Kumiko turned her attentions to the other foot, Lauren felt her legs begin to tingle like the aftershock of an orgasm. The pleasure spread along her nerve endings and she gasped as her sex began to pulse in response. It was intoxicating. Every bit of it.

Seeing the effect her ministrations were having, Kumiko looked up at Lauren with an impish little smile. 'Wanna play?'

A hot blush painted Lauren's cheeks and she bit her lip. God, yes, she did want to play.

Without waiting for a reply, Kumiko lowered her head and kissed Lauren's foot. Her lips closed gently over the big toe and her tongue swirled in circles around it as though it were a tiny penis. The soft warm folds of her mouth felt like silk.

Lauren held perfectly still, not wanting to do anything to disrupt the moment. Her hands clutched the arms of the chair and she pressed her bottom down hard into the seat. She had never imagined that her feet could be so sensitive, so responsive. It felt like she was being brought back to life.

Kumiko began to kiss, lick and suck the other toes, her tongue seeking and teasing the delicate webbing between them before sliding up and over the instep. Then she raised Lauren's leg so she could kiss the soft flesh of her sole.

Lauren could feel her knickers growing damp as she surrendered to the blissful sensations. It crossed her mind to wonder whether the cherry-scented oil was some sort of aphrodisiac. Not that it was even necessary. Kumiko was quite possibly the most beautiful thing Lauren had ever seen. She had felt seduced since the girl had chased her down and lured her to the salon. Lauren was smitten by her physical allure, her sexy voice and now her talented tongue. She allowed her legs to fall open and she closed her eyes as she imagined the other areas Kumiko could pleasure.

The girl's fingers trailed up along the insides of Lauren's legs, edging teasingly close to the lacy edge of her knickers only to dance away. Lauren met her eyes with a pleading look and Kumiko pressed a finger to Lauren's lips. Greedily Lauren kissed it and tasted cherries. With a sigh of pleasure, she sucked the finger into her mouth, swirling her tongue round it as Kumiko had done with her toes.

Immediately she felt suffused with warmth and her breathing grew deeper and heavier as Kumiko slipped back down to lavish attention on her other foot. Lauren pointed her toes obligingly and Kumiko smiled as she fluttered her tongue against them, drawing them into her mouth one at a time, lapping the cherry-flavoured oil off them.

Lauren's sex ached with need and she found herself grinding her hips into the chair. When she couldn't take any more she lifted her free leg and wrapped it around Kumiko's back, pulling her in closer. With a final flick of her tongue, Kumiko released Lauren's foot and kissed a trail up the inside of her leg. She pushed the edge of the skirt out of her way and slid an oily finger along the damp gusset of Lauren's knickers. Lauren gasped as pleasure surged through her like an electric shock, setting her whole body on fire. Then she raised her bottom up so Kumiko could slip her fingers into the waistband of her knickers and slide them down.

Kumiko turned away and dropped the sodden scrap of lace onto a little table and Lauren whimpered at her momentary absence. She was so desperate for more that the seconds Kumiko was away felt like abandonment. But in no time Kumiko was back and Lauren released a long shuddering breath as the Japanese girl placed her hands on Lauren's thighs and spread her legs wide apart until they were draped over the arms of the chair and she was displayed fully, lewdly.

Heat spread through her body at the thought of how she must look, but it only made her hotter. She wanted Kumiko to see all of her, to touch and taste all of her.

'So pretty,' Kumiko murmured as her soft fingers traced lazy circles around Lauren's sex. 'Just like the petals of an orchid.' She plucked one of the flowers from the basin to show Lauren. She stroked it suggestively before drawing its quivering pink petals along the damp lips of Lauren's sex. 'Both so delicate, so lovely, so open. Everything on display, nothing hidden.'

Lauren held her breath, savouring the sensation as the cool petals of the flower caressed her lips and teased the warm wet opening of her pussy.

'Please,' she panted, unable to say more than that.

Kumiko let go of the blossom, placed her fingers on either side of the swollen, hungry lips and splayed them open, then slid her thumbs up and down along the slick folds with excruciating deliberation. Lauren could only writhe and whimper pleadingly at each jolt of sensation. She wanted Kumiko's fingers inside her. Or better still, her soft pink tongue.

But Kumiko clearly had her own plans and Lauren groaned in protest as she felt the other girl's fingers lift away from her sex. Kumiko planted her knee between Lauren's spread legs, pushed firmly up against her pussy and smiled at the little moan the action produced. Then she leaned forwards and hauled the front of Lauren's jumper up past her breasts and over her head, revealing her lacy white demi-bra. Kumiko lightly stroked the swell of cleavage before easing Lauren's breasts out of the cups, exposing her nipples. They were hard as pebbles. Lauren blushed at the exposure, her arms clothed, her bare breasts and sex on display, her desire blatant and shameless.

Kumiko slid her cherry-scented fingers over Lauren's nipples, lightly at first, then with a little more firmness. She stroked and pinched them while Lauren's breathing quickened and her heart began to race.

She stared in wonderment at the beautiful girl inflicting such incredible sensations on her. No man had ever stimulated her this much, least of all her husband. She had to laugh to herself at the thought of Jake. How many times had he (only half-jokingly) hinted that they should try a threesome? What would he think if he could see her now? A sudden flash of possessiveness surprised her; she would never share Kumiko with him. There was something pure and almost innocent about this stolen moment, something that shouldn't be defiled by the crass ogling of her boorish husband.

Kumiko's warm mouth banished all thoughts of Jake, and Lauren closed her eyes, losing herself in the wet heat of another girl's tongue circling her nipples, one at a time. Kumiko was focused, deliberate, brushing her velvety lips across one stiff little peak while teasing the other with a gentle finger. She closed her lips over one as she pinched the other, then switched so that each side received the same treatment. And all the while she kissed, touched and licked, she continued to press her knee against Lauren's sex, grinding it very slowly and very gently.

Lauren realised she'd been gripping the chair as if holding on for dear life. She let go and reached for her lover, burying her hands in the silky curtain of jet-black hair. Kumiko responded with a flick of her tongue against Lauren's nipple. With a gasp, Lauren threw her head back, the delicious sensation ricocheting through her body.

When Lauren didn't think she could handle any more teasing, Kumiko finally raised her head. She met Lauren's eyes and she seemed to like the frenzied lust she saw there. She smiled again and slipped her hand down between Lauren's thighs and up to the place that wanted her attention the most. A finger teased her again before sliding easily inside. At the same time, Kumiko pressed her lips to Lauren's and the sweet taste of her was so welcome it was almost overpowering.

Lauren sucked Kumiko's tongue into her mouth and swirled her own round and round it as if they were dancing. Then she clutched fistfuls of Kumiko's glossy black hair as she ground her hips against the finger, asking, *begging* for more.

At last Kumiko broke the kiss and slid down to her knees again, withdrawing her finger. And by the time she finally dipped her head and pressed her mouth against the dewy little slit that was aching for her, Lauren was so over-stimulated that she knew it would only be a matter of seconds. The chair creaked as she clutched the arms again and her thighs began to tremble with the effort of holding herself open and spread.

Kumiko's tongue moved languidly over the folds and creases of Lauren's sex, eliciting little cries and gasps. It was electrifying. Without question the most intense stimuli she had ever experienced in her life. Even her vibrator couldn't compete. The pleasure was almost unbearable.

With tiny flickering movements, Kumiko teased the hard nub of her clit, alternately kissing it and sucking it into her mouth. Lauren tossed her head from side to side, completely at the mercy of the rising waves of ecstasy. And when Kumiko slipped her finger back inside, the sensual onslaught finally proved too much for Lauren. She came fast and hard, biting her arm to keep from screaming.

The orgasm left her spent, gasping and panting. She was in a state of total disarray, her legs splayed obscenely to reveal her dripping sex, her breasts exposed and the nipples glistening with cherry oil. It took her some time to recover enough to move and by then her legs had started to go numb. The pins and needles shocked her back to the real world and she adjusted her bra and her jumper with shaky hands, not knowing what to say.

Her face was flushed with more than just satisfaction and it was several minutes before she was able to meet Kumiko's eyes. The girl was grinning broadly.

'I've never done that before,' Lauren said at last, just for something to fill the silence.

'With a woman, you mean.'

'Um, yes. With a woman.' Lauren laughed, then thought about what she'd just said and corrected herself. 'No, actually, not with *anyone*. That was just … incredible.'

Now it was Kumiko's turn to blush. 'You probably think I do this with all my clients, right? But it was my first time too. I just – your feet were so beautiful and when I saw how you were responding – well, I guess I just couldn't help myself.'

Lauren looked down at her feet, still surprised that they could hold any erotic appeal for anyone.

'I can't wait to show you how beautiful they can be,' Kumiko said, rising to her feet as though she was ready to get to work.

Lauren stopped her with a hand against her chest. 'Maybe not just yet,' she said. One by one she slowly unfastened the buttons of Kumiko's blouse and the purple silk parted liquidly over her skin to reveal her bare breasts. They were small, barely a handful, and Lauren felt an answering tingle in her own breasts as she cupped Kumiko's, squeezed them gently and then teased the nipples into stiffness. Lauren bent down to kiss them.

Kumiko moaned softly and trembled and Lauren slid the tight black skirt up over her hips. Then she sank to her knees on the floor before her and smiled as she saw that Kumiko wore no panties.

'Kinky girl,' Lauren murmured as she traced a sinuous line up Kumiko's thigh and teased her sex with fleeting touches that made her gasp.

'Oh yes,' Kumiko sighed. 'Very kinky.'

Lauren imagined the beautiful Japanese girl spending her working days sitting before the objects of her lust, fantasising about the perfect feet as she pressed her bare thighs together beneath her clothes. Did she go home frustrated? Did she sprawl naked on her bed and pleasure herself with toys? Or lie back in the bath and treat herself to a barrage of water from the shower massager?

The pictures in Lauren's mind were making her wet again and she pressed her lips to Kumiko's delicate pink sex. She lapped softly with her tongue at first, tasting her sweet hot wetness. Kumiko sighed with pleasure and her legs shook with the effort of holding herself up as Lauren closed her lips around her clit. She nipped gently, making Kumiko gasp, then swirled her tongue in vigorous circles around the sensitive spot. It was all Kumiko could do to stay on her feet and Lauren clasped the girl's buttocks to hold her steady.

She continued the assault with her tongue until Kumiko cried out and plunged her hands into Lauren's hair as her body went rigid and then limp. Lauren caught her in her arms and held her, inhaling the rich exotic scent of her perfume mingled with the cherry oil.

When they finally broke apart they shared a bashful smile. Lauren could hardly believe what she'd done and what she'd allowed to be done to her. Neither of them spoke as Kumiko tidied herself up and then filed, polished and photographed Lauren's feet. There was no need for words.

* * *

Two weeks later, Lauren was at the mall with Jake and her heart gave a little flutter as they walked past the Beauty and Serenity salon. But it was the poster in the window that made her stop and stare.

A vivid colour photograph of her pedicured feet took up almost the whole of the glass. The high arches were shown to their best advantage, with one foot pointed provocatively across the instep of the other. As though the feet themselves were secret lovers and the glossy red toenails were lips puckering for a kiss. An orchid was nestled between the toes of the top foot, its vivid pink petals splayed lasciviously.

Lauren swallowed. Her sex tingled in response to the memories triggered by the image and she managed to get hold of herself.

'Nice,' she said casually.

Jake looked at the poster and shrugged. 'S'pose so,' he said with a grunt. He hadn't even recognised his wife's feet.

'He'll be kissing your feet after one of our special pedicures,' the poster proclaimed in elegant script beneath the picture. Lauren knew that wasn't exactly the case. At least not where her husband was concerned. Jake might not have any special appreciation for her feet but she knew someone who did.

She remembered Kumiko placing the orchid between her toes and stroking the petals before setting up the camera to take the picture. She thought she could feel her smooth fingers now, soft as petals themselves. Caressing her sex, teasing her and making her want more. A little moan escaped her.

Jake glanced at her and then down at his watch, clearly unaware of the heat building between her legs. He was only impatient to leave.

Lauren gave him a chaste little kiss on the cheek. 'Listen,' she said, 'why don't you go on home and watch the game? I think I'll just pop into the salon for a couple of hours. I wouldn't mind a little footie match of my own.'

A Little Light Relief
(Dialogue between Myself and a Cunty Businessman)
Willow Sears

Me: Are you going to gawp at my tits all night?

CB   *(spluttering on his whiskey)*: I wasn't! I haven't been –

Me: Since you got here you've either been eyeing up the barmaid or sneaking glances at my chest. And I bet you had a good old look at my arse when I went to powder my nose.

CB   *(like a puffed-up cockerel)*: Miss, I can assure you that –

Me: I guess with what I'm wearing I should expect some attention, but it's a bit presumptuous of you, don't you think? I mean, you aren't that bad looking for someone who must be nearly old enough to be my father. And you have nice shoes, I guess, and shorter hair is always a good idea for men thinning on top. But you're not exactly in peak physical condition, are you? You are a bit paunchy around the middle and you've got as many chins as you have measures of whiskey in that glass.

CB *(incredulous)*: It's only a double!

Me: Precisely. So, presumptuous then; you clearly fancy your chances with me even though you are a bit old and a bit saggy and undoubtedly past your prime. Whereas I, without being too narcissistic, look pretty fucking gorgeous. You agree, I trust?

CB *(quite taken aback)*: Well, if you are fishing for compliments, then yes, you are very attractive and, yes, it's hard not to stare at your backside when it looks so compelling squashed against that barstool.

Me: So no doubt you have been thinking about bending me over it. Just a fuck, was it, or were you imagining giving me a little spanking first? That's a nice tie, by the way. Are you wearing it for a bet?

CB *(perplexed, head swimming)*: What? It's my favourite tie! My wife bought it for me!

Me: It's lovely. I always find cartoon characters on clothing so hilarious. The red of Winnie the Pooh's jacket matches your eyes a treat. I assume that you are here hoping for some extramarital fun?

CB *(trying to look offended)*: I'm here because I am down on business. I'm staying a few doors away at the Regent and the bar there is like a morgue. I came in here for a quiet drink, that's all.

Me: And no doubt your business colleagues are all fat, boring bastards who don't recognise a golden opportunity when they see one?

CB *(with a knowing smirk)*: Well ...

Me: Whereas in here there is me, and I am a lonesome beauty with a truly delicious arse. And you're thinking that any young girl dressed in a skin-tight electric-blue catsuit, sat alone in a bar at nearly one o'clock in the morning, has either been stood up or must be really desperate. Either that or she is most likely a whore. Am I right?

CB *(allowing himself another misguided smirk)*: Well, I never said that ...

Me: Good, because any man who calls me a whore gets his cock ripped off.

CB *(in a chastised, back-to-square-one-after-thinking-he-was-getting-somewhere-with-me kind of way)*: Now wait, I wasn't suggesting for one minute –

Me: I am neither desperate nor a cheap tart, and I think the likelihood of me ever getting stood up is infinitesimally slim. Not that it's any of your business but I've been to a fetish club to strap-on-fuck a couple of fine arses, which is why I'm dressed this way. And I'm now here because I *own* this place and because I have to come back to keep an eye on that sneaky bitch barmaid down there who would drink away all the profits in a flash if I let her. I don't pay my bar girls, you see. All they earn is tips, and if I wasn't here she would be doing anything to earn some, including giving out freebies. Plus she is the most insatiable slut I have ever met. She might look all sweet and innocent down there twirling her hair around her finger and reading her magazine, but if I wasn't here she would be trying *anything* to get herself some pleasure. Since she's my girlfriend as well as my employee, I simply cannot tolerate that. Your trousers are bulging, by the way.

CB *(flushed and flustered, hastily pulling at his crotch to hide the swelling within)*: It's just the way they … I'm not, erm … So why do they stay then, if you don't pay?

Me: Oh, I make certain they get plenty of money. And that one is such a filthy minx she will do anything to earn it – which, I guess, *does* make her a whore. She is the least faithful girlfriend I have ever had but she absolutely worships me and I do so love to spank her chubby backside. Is that as big as your bulge gets, by the way? It's not very impressive, is it?

CB *(face like a slapped haddock)*: What?

Me: Pretty soon I'm going to have to pop upstairs for a little light relief and I'm afraid to leave her down here alone. That cosy foursome tucked around the corner won't be up for any of her tricks but I wouldn't trust you as far as I could throw you, even if you aren't exactly packing the prize-winning marrow down there.

CB *(incredulous again – he does it so well)*: I'll have you know there is nothing wrong with the size of my –

Me: I have to go to great lengths to ensure she behaves. One time I fitted a chastity belt on her. I only left her for the day. She went to a locksmith and had it cut free! She ended up fucking the locksmith and his assistant for their trouble. She came home to me with both her holes still dripping. Can you believe it? Only nineteen years old and she's already had a double stuffing! Dirty bitch. This is why I can't trust her with *anyone*, you see? Before I left tonight I made her stuff her knickers up inside her cunt, which hopefully kept her out of trouble. She has such a delicious, velvet-smooth cunt – you should feel it. It's so unbelievably tight, considering how she likes to abuse it. I came down one time and found her stretching herself open with a wine bottle – and I'm not talking the neck end either. It's all down to her pussy juice, I reckon. It is the sweetest, slickest cream you could imagine. It is so slippery that it lets anything inside her, no matter how tight she is. And there is so much of it too! The boys all say that having their balls bathed in her cream is one of the Wonders of the World. And she loves to do it for them too. Any cock will do for her, which is why I have to go out of my way to make sure she isn't cheating on me. For instance, she's due a break in a minute. I'm going to have to take her into the restroom, bend her over in the cubicle and pour a whole bottle of cold beer into her arse. She will have to hold it inside while I give her puss a slow, gentle rubbing. If she lasts ten minutes I will let her come, and while she does so she will be allowed to spurt all the beer back out into the toilet. Then I will tug the knickers out of her cunt and make her put them on. That will make her behave while I'm away. Her climax will be hard enough to keep her satisfied for some time, and not even *she* would try it on with anyone while wearing come-saturated underwear and with beer still trickling out of her arse. So how much have you got?

CB *(open-mouthed, wide-eyed, visibly trembling)*: What – *inches*?

Me: No, not inches, you idiot – *money*. You thought I was a whore and you were undoubtedly toying with the idea of fucking me, so how much did you think I would charge? How much did you think I was worth? How much have you got on you? Or did you think I would do you for free?

CB *(stammering, and it's the haddock face again. Or is it a cod? It's so hard to tell)*: I'm not sure, around two hundred, I guess.

Me: Wow, a whole two hundred pounds! Did you want my mouth for that too, or did you just think you would get my pussy? Do you like freshly shaved

cunts or would you use my sparseness to try to nego-
tiate a discount? You can't have thought you would
get my arse for that too? It's such a tight virgin hole
I just don't think I could give it away so cheaply.

CB *(shifting in his seat, flushed and looking like he might
have some kind of underwear accident at any second)*:
Well, I wouldn't say no to your arse if it was –

Me: Gosh, two whole hundred for maybe only an hour's
work, and all I would have to do is close my eyes
and give up my soul, surrender my luscious body to
a middle-aged flabby man with a cock shortage.

CB *(confused and offended, but unable to jump from his
seat while trying to adjust the uncomfortably swelling member inside his trousers)*: Look, I never said
you were a –

Me: She, on the other hand – that smug slut perched
down the end of the bar who is meant to be my girlfriend – *she* would give you anything for two hundred, and not even bat an eyelid. She would give you
tits, mouth, pussy and arse. She would even give
you change. Is your cock leaking? You seem to be
in some discomfort. *She* would let you do whatever
you wanted to her for only half that amount. That's
not a bad thought, is it? For a meagre hundred you
could get to do the dirtiest things you could dream
up, with very probably the sexiest girl you could
ever get to fuck. The sky is literally the limit with

her. You are bounded only by the extent of your imagination. I mean, I'm not trying to put ideas into your head, but, if you were to do her from behind, she really does like you to slip your thumb up into her arse. As long as you've made it all wet first. Or, once she's got your cock all coated in her luscious cream, you could do a lot worse than to take it out and slap her bum cheeks with it, or maybe wipe it all over her face. And you should call her a few filthy bitch names too, especially when she stops sucking your balls to stick her tongue up your arse. She always has her fingers stuffed up her cunt when she does this, so insults aren't usually hard to come by. So, what *would* you ask of her, bearing in mind she would give you anything?

CB (*flustered, losing a couple of pounds in sweat, trying to sound reasonable even though he is about to discuss with a complete stranger exactly which perversions he would like to perform on a teenager*): Well, her arse is lovely, so I wouldn't mind –

Me: It *is* a nice arse, soft but not too big. She's so very pretty too. I think one of the sexiest sights is that of a very pretty girl having her bum-hole licked. That's all you would ask? You could get anything, you know. I once came back and some blonde MILF with really big tits had lured her into the restroom. Do you know what *she* asked her to do? Fucking filthy bitch, I bet her tits weren't even real. She said – sorry, are you OK? You look like you are sitting on a snake. Do you need another drink? You know what that filthy MILF said to my girlfriend? She said, 'Piss for me.' It's true, I heard it! I was right outside the cubicle and she said to my girlfriend, 'Do it for me now and I will let you come.' Can you believe that? What a disgusting cunt! That's like something a man would say, not some woman in her forties, even if she did have falsies. Still, at least she aimed high. She could see my girlfriend was a ravenous slut so she tried to go the whole hog. You might only get one such opportunity in your whole life so it's best to try your luck. And she would have got what she wanted too. That bitch was sat backwards on the can with her arse stuck out, squeezing away. I dragged the woman by her hair to the flat upstairs and used my fists on her. It was probably the roughest I have ever been. I don't think she knew what hit her. Actually, she *did* get exactly what she wanted, if I remember rightly, although I don't think she necessarily wanted it while my naughty girlfriend was sat on top of her fat tits, spanking her sopping MILF cunt. And that's not the only time I've walked in on my so-called girlfriend while she's been betraying me. I witnessed her taking a jizz-bomb another time. I swear I was only gone ten minutes and when I came back five guys were spunking all over her face and bare breasts. She must have been on her knees within thirty seconds of me leaving. It was all in her hair and up her nose. I had to send her straight home to clean up. The worse thing was the speed they did it. It left her gagging in more ways than one! I hate men who come too quick. I bet you are like that.

CB *(wanting to get up and go, but unable to drag himself away; practically cross-eyed with excitement, squirming like his cock might go off at any second and make a mockery of his denials)*: No way! Older men *do* learn a thing or two –

Me: You know, if I'm being really honest, I don't think I would mind any man doing anything to my slutty girlfriend, as long as they were able to last long enough. The trouble is she is just so filthy it gets them all spurting as soon as they've got their cocks out, and that just gets her all hot and wanting more. I've learned my lesson though. Now I absolutely insist that any man who fucks her jerks himself off first.

CB *(with quizzical grin)*: So you would let a stranger fuck your girlfriend?

Me: It's not as weird as you think. She is absolutely insatiable and will always want cock. If I let a man fuck her, as long as he lasts ages and gives it to her really hard, at least he can fuck some of the fire out of her. That way, when it's my turn, I can take what I want

64

and still get some sleep without her bugging me for more. He has to last though. Quick comers are no good to me. If they only give her ten minutes I will be up all night with her, trying to think of dirtier and dirtier ways to satisfy her and get her off to sleep. I have heard guys claim they can go all night but, once they are inside her gorgeous body and listening to her screams and dirty talk, they shoot within minutes. That's why I insist they empty their balls before they take her on. Actually, I wouldn't mind someone stepping up to the plate tonight, because just the thought of her endlessly rubbing her dripping cunt all over my face and body is making me exhausted.

CB *(red-faced and animated)*: So, if I came in my trousers right now, would you let me fuck her?

Me: Came in your trousers? Isn't that what little boys do? No, that will never do. Kirsty, come here, baby. This man wants to fuck you but I don't think he has a very big cock. Tell Kirsty what your name is.

CB *(spluttering again)*: It's Michael and there's nothing wrong with the size of my –

Me: Michael what? Don't you think she should know before you stick your cock up her arse?

CB *(with just slight hesitation)*: It's Haines, Michael Haines. Why do you keep saying I've got a small –

Me: It's your lucky day, Pin Prick. If you want to fuck her then it is quite simple. You just have to take your cock out right now and let us watch you come. Once you have done that, presuming you are man enough to get it up again, you can do whatever you like to her. As long as you don't mind me watching and playing with myself, that is.

CB *(crimson-faced and wet-lipped)*: You're shitting me! No way – you are just teasing. What do you mean, take my cock out? I can't do it here, can I?

Me: You most certainly can, Mikey-Boy. Just whip it out and toss yourself off and then we can all get down to some business. To be perfectly frank, I'm completely bushed and need all the help I can get with her tonight. I've had men jerk off at the bar before. It's perfectly safe. That lot sitting around there can't see you, and they are way too drunk to care what you are doing anyway. You can't see the bar from outside and nobody is coming in at this hour. It's a bit of a test, you see, a trial to decide whether you are fit to fill my girlfriend's scrumptious bum. Anyway, I don't believe you have even a normal-sized cock, despite your claims to the contrary. It's your chance to prove me wrong.

CB *(wild-eyed and wondering how it has suddenly progressed from him being generally abused and tormented to being offered my girlfriend's arse on a plate)*: There's no way I'm going to fall for ... I don't know what your game is but –

Me: I do believe he is going to get his cock out for us, Kirsty.

CB *(sneering now, like a final defiance in the face of his executioner)*: You fucking dirty bitch, what are you up to, you prick-teasing slut?

Me: And there it is! Go on, spit on it and give it a good wanking. That's it: the faster you come, the faster you can shit-poke my Kirsty's sexy arse.

CB *(open-mouthed and panting)*: You fucking bitch ... You fucking ... *bitch!*

Me: Come on now, stroke that tool for us. I hope it gets bigger than that, don't you, Kirsty? Perhaps it's the stage-fright. Are you nervous? Is it going to get any bigger? Most guys would be spraying by now. Is it because you are old? Would you like us to take off our clothes and bend over, show you our lovely tight little arses? Would that make it easier for you? We'd both love to feel your hot come shooting onto our shit-holes. Wank it faster, come on, show us your spunk!

CB *(eyes screwing shut then opening wide, mouth agape and gasping as I bend forward to spit thickly on his cockhead to give him some extra lube)*: Ah, yes! You dirty whore ... You fucking filthy cunt ...

Me: You're nearly there, granddad! Go on, tell Kirsty what you are going to do to her!

CB *(panting away and just basically pulling a string of laughable pre-orgasm faces)*: I'm going to fuck your sexy bitch arse! I'm going to fuck the shit out of you!

Me: Yes, I'm not actually sure it's long enough to reach her shit, let alone fuck it out of her. Never mind, keep going! Your balls are tightening – you're ready to blow! Do it all over yourself, Mikey-Boy, we want to see you covered in your own spunk!

CB *(beetroot-faced and grimacing risibly)*: You fu– You dirty cu– Ah! Shit! *Aaahhhh!*

Me: Yes, spray it for us, show us your nasty spunk fountain. Soak yourself with it. Keep wanking – we want to see every last drop.

CB *(chest heaving as he tries to regain his composure, spent but triumphant, a contented smile on his lips)*: You bitches are going to have to suck me good and proper to get me hard again, or are you scared of taking a proper cock inside you?

Me: Well, much as we would love to have your fine, below-average, piss-smelling cock in our private places, there is something we would like from you even more.

CB *(still panting but now edgy, sensing his chance evaporating with his post-climax indolence, guessing the double-cross)*: What the fuck are you talking about?

Me: There is nothing that turns me on more than the sight of a grown man humiliating himself. I love to use my power to sap them of theirs. It makes me *so* fucking horny. Kirsty, go upstairs and get naked and wait for me. And make sure you squirt a whole bottle of baby oil into your backside because I've got a very long dildo waiting for you.

CB *(even he knows he sounds ridiculous)*: Hold on, you *are* going to let me fuck her, right?

Me: Well, not exactly. Like I said, I want something else from you. You see that black circle up there, above the optics? It's a security camera. It's been trained on you since I went off to powder my nose. I'm thinking of sending a copy of the tape to your wife. Unless, of course …

CB *(face darkening with his mood and high blood pressure, going beyond beetroot and heading towards the colour of purple sprouting broccoli)*: Why the hell would you want to do that? What the fuck have I done to you? *(Laughs)* You're having me on, aren't you? It's a joke, right?*(Panicky again)* You stupid bitch, you can't send any tape when you don't even know where I live!

Me: The hotel does though, doesn't it? The Regent Hotel, didn't you say? I have a long-standing agreement with that particular establishment, as it happens. You would have given your details at the reception desk, wouldn't you, Mr Haines? I've just made you wank off in public with nothing more than an empty promise, so how long do you think it would take me to persuade the concierge to part with this information?

CB *(exasperated and defeated, a little whiny in fact)*: You twisted bitch. Why ever would you do that? What the hell do you want from me?

Me: A tip, that's all, nothing more. Just a tip for my barmaid to keep her happy and to keep her in sexy underwear. One small tip and then you can walk away, go back home and keep this evening to yourself, forget it ever happened.

CB *(trying to do incredulous again but too hollow now to make it work)*: You complete fu– You just … How much are you talking about? How *much* of a tip?

Me: Oh, only a little one. Let's say about two hundred.

CB *(aghast)*: *Two hundred?* What did she do that was worth all that?

Me: It's not so much what *she* is worth, Mr Haines. It is what your *marriage* is worth – a trifling amount when you look at it like that. If you want to act the bastard when you are away, then be prepared to pay for it. You should expect a little solidarity from us females when you males are all such unscrupulous, cheating fucks! And stop moaning. You probably waste hundreds of pounds on those sex-chat lines and never get anything close to what I've just given you. You have just got your cock out and been allowed to come in front of two of the sexiest girls you will ever see in your life. It's hardly the end of the world, is it?

CB *(pointlessly)*: You *tricked* me. There – two hundred fucking pounds, you thieving, conniving, *cunting* bitch!

Me: Thank you, I shall see that Kirsty gets it. Now, Mr Haines, it's very late and there is a soft, spankable bottom waiting upstairs for me to abuse, so why don't you try to wipe some of that filthy spunk off the front of your trousers, drink your drink and then get the fuck out of my bar.

Me *(To no one in particular)*: Well, that was easy!

Fast and Easy
Lolita Lopez

Like waves rolling across the ocean, a sea of bodies
undulated on the concrete dancefloor and swept Alix up
in their sensual, free-flowing current. She gyrated to the
hypnotic techno beats echoing off the metal walls of the
vacant warehouse. Above her, yards of white silk dripped
from the rafters and billowed in the powerful breeze of
high-velocity fans mounted along the ceiling. Flashing
strobe lights created the illusion of slow, choppy movements among her fellow dancers. Black lights provided
the only constant source of illumination in the makeshift
nightclub. The purple glow highlighted the neon murals
covering the wall and the party sponsors' foam logos
scrawled across the dancefloor.

Like Alix, most of the women wore short, flashy skirts
paired with bikini tops, the damp fabric clinging to their
curves and enticing their male counterparts. Among the

men, board shirts and tees seemed to be the preferred clothing for the night. It was a smart choice considering that an hour ago thick pastel-tinted foam had coated everyone on the dancefloor from head to toe.

Now the remnants of the slick mixture clung to the hot bodies of the tightly packed dancers. Alix's bare skin felt slightly sticky as her sweat mixed with the deflated suds. All around her, people writhed in hedonistic pleasure. She submitted fully to the heady experience, allowing unknown men and women to grope and clutch at her. Their strange hands roamed her body. At first, she'd found the sensation a bit off-putting and frightening but, as she embraced the rather decadent experience, she discovered she enjoyed the illicit thrill of being pawed by unknown people.

As the party reached its climax, the building pulsed with raw sexuality. Everywhere she looked, couples and even larger groups of dancers were getting frisky. There were elbows crooked around necks and hands grasping bare thighs. Fingers gripped hips. Palms cupped breasts. Throbbing erections strained to break free from their cloth constraints as couples ground their bodies together.

In the centre of the pulsing throng, Alix slowly realised she commanded the hungry gaze of every lusting person surrounding her. She wondered what it was that they all liked. Her dark hair? Her naturally pouty mouth? Those green eyes she'd inherited from her father or the voluptuous swing of her hips she'd got from her mother's genes? Maybe it was all or even none of those things. She didn't really care. It was just nice to be the centre of attention.

With the deafening thud of the music as her metronome, Alix swivelled her hips and swung her arms overhead, fully aware that lifting her arms displayed her ample cleavage at its best. She caught the dark gaze of a man she'd been watching all night. Stocky and average height, he stared intently, his gaze raking her body as if to memorise every curve. His close-cropped haircut gave him away but, if there'd been any doubt, the red T-shirt emblazoned with the USMC logo hugging his muscular arms and chest sealed the deal.

Alix sized him up as she shimmied and dropped. She'd seen her fair share of drop-dead-sexy frat boys over the last four years of college, but this Marine blew them out of the water. He had the look of a man. Confident, mature and utterly delicious, there was no boyish softness to his face. Lean, tight, handsome – her fingers just itched to touch him.

Thrilled by the idea of taking a Marine for a test drive, Alix boldly lifted a hand and crooked her finger in his direction. She beckoned him closer with a come-hither motion and an enticing smile. Just as she'd anticipated, he grinned and obeyed her silent command, cutting across the packed floor until he stood in front of her. For a long moment, they simply stared at one another. She sensed he wasn't sure who should make the first move.

With a sly smile, Alix spun around and backed up against him. His body heat penetrated her skin and left her feeling relaxed and secure. His thickly corded arms encircled her waist, and he pulled her tight to his chest. Excitement surged through her. A blistering warmth rushed through her core. With his hands grasping her hips, Alix rocked with him in time to the incessant thump of the music. Beads of sweat slicked their skin as the temperature in the warehouse rose higher and higher despite the fans. She didn't pull away in search of cooler air but pressed harder against him, grinding her ass against the rock-hard erection barely contained by his shorts.

He grew more daring and slid his hands along the baby-soft skin of her bare stomach. His rough, callused fingers elicited little shivers as they stroked her naked skin. His hands drifted higher and his fingers paused just under the swell of her breasts. He played with the gold fabric of her bikini top and lightly scratched her midriff.

Eyes closed, Alix enjoyed the way his hands felt on her body. His touch awakened her sultry side and left her desperate for more of him. Always the coquette, Alix raised her arms and hooked her wrists behind his neck, drawing his chin down to the curve of her throat. She turned her face and nuzzled his ear. 'My name is Alix.'

He lifted his head and pressed his lips to her ear. 'Mitch.'

She shuddered as his teeth grazed the shell of her ear and playfully bit down on her earlobe. His lips trailed featherlight kisses along her neck before he pressed them to her shoulder. She shuddered as his hands followed the sloping plane of her belly. Insistently, they reached the pivotal point of decency as they slipped beneath her skirt. She didn't even try to stop him. Her arousal skyrocketed as he stoked the flames of lust burning low and hot in her belly.

No longer content with dancing and groping, Alix searched for a shadowy corner, a doorway to another room, somewhere, anywhere, that she might lead him. All she needed was a sense of privacy, a place where she might feel protected from prying eyes. As her gaze jumped around the warehouse, she spotted a couple who didn't seem to share her threshold for modesty. Her eyes widened at the sight of the girl straddling her man's lap and riding him as if he were a racing stallion.

Her gaze lingered on the salacious sight a moment too long, and Mitch caught her watching the couple. His amused laugh rumbled through her chest. 'They look like they're having fun.'

'Yes,' she answered breathlessly as he nibbled her neck.

'Maybe we should find a little place where we can have some fun.' His searching fingers found their way under the scrap of fabric shielding her sex and dipped between the soft folds of her pussy. She gasped as his finger found and circled her clit. Her thighs tensed and toes curled as she tried to maintain composure on the dancefloor.

Nipples tight and pussy pulsing with need, she desperately glanced around the warehouse. Aha! Alix spotted a sliver of light across the warehouse as a door swung open and closed again and again. She watched a trickle of women entering and exiting and realised it was a bathroom. Perfect!

Alix grasped Mitch's wrist and dragged his hand from her panties. She pivoted to face him and wrapped her arms around his shoulders. She tugged down his head and trailed her fingertips along the slight stubble outlining his square jaw before claiming his mouth in a slow, sensual kiss. As their tongues darted and circled, Mitch's growing erection stabbed at her navel. Already weak-kneed and aching for more intimate contact, Alix encouraged his desire by grazing her fingers along his lower stomach. She let her hand slide lower and squeezed his fat cock through his shorts. His dick pulsed beneath her touch, and she smiled naughtily. 'Come with me.'

He gladly yielded to her as she abandoned his cock and took his hand instead. Like a puppy desperate to please its new mistress, he happily followed her through the crowd. They weaved in and out of the dancing throng, pausing here and there to avoid collisions. As they neared the bathroom, she started to lose her nerve as her lust-filled mind cleared a bit. Was she really dragging a stranger into a warehouse bathroom for a quickie?

Yes. The answer raced through her mind fast and clear. She absolutely was. In all her life she'd rarely done the wrong thing, but tonight? Oh, tonight she wanted to be really, really bad.

Although dimly lit, the bathroom was surprisingly clean and contained two rows of stalls and only a handful of occupants. Not a second glance was given to Alix and Mitch as they entered. The girls were much too busy fixing makeup, indulging illicit drug habits or gossiping loudly about their romantic rivals. The sight of a man in their midst garnered little more than a passive smile of acknowledgement. When Alix spotted a dishevelled and flushed couple exiting one of the stalls, she understood why. Apparently the restroom had become an unofficial hookup spot. It wasn't the sexiest of places, but it served its purpose.

As soon as they were locked in the first available stall, Alix pounced on Mitch. Not wanting to lose her nerve, she smothered him with kisses. The bitterness of Mexican beer, the bright bite of lime and a tinge of salt teased her taste-buds. Mitch feverishly returned her kisses. He stabbed his tongue between her lips and tangled his long fingers in her hair. She gasped as he grabbed a handful of her locks and tugged hard enough to tip her chin towards the ceiling. Mitch's mouth descended on her exposed neck, his teeth scraping and lips sucking hard. She shivered under his intense ministrations and prayed her wobbly knees would keep her upright.

Mitch expertly unsnapped the hook at the back of her neck, sending the fabric of her halter-style bikini plummeting towards her belly button. Breasts bared to him, Alix licked her lips and grasped his hands. She placed them on her body and moaned as he squeezed the full roundness of her flesh. He bent low to capture her nipple between his lips. His spicy citrus cologne invaded her nose and left her feeling intoxicated. She inhaled deeply as his mouth tugged on her nipple and sent quivering shocks straight to her clit.

Alix groaned loudly as he teased her other breast. He pinched and rolled her abandoned, wet nipple until her toes were curling. She bucked against his body in a wild attempt to assuage the burning need between her thighs.

In one fluid motion, Mitch sank to the tile floor. He grasped the backs of her thighs and lifted her legs until her knees draped over his broad shoulders. She shook with excitement and anticipation as he kissed her inner thighs and slowly gathered the ruffles of her skirt in his hands. He tucked the excess fabric into the waistband, revealing the tiny scrap of cloth covering her pussy, then tugged on the simple knots sitting low on her hips and freed her from the bikini bottom. She didn't even protest when he dropped it on the bathroom floor. It was a small sacrifice to the pleasure that was sure to come.

She widened her thighs atop his shoulders and stared down at him as he used his thumbs to part the pink petals of her sex. He smiled with appreciation as he gazed at her dewy folds. Teasingly slow, he dragged his tongue along the length of her slit before swirling the tip around her clit. She moaned as he deftly flicked the little pearl. Side to side and up and down, he alternated strokes of his tongue with gentle suckling. He drove her crazy as he ate her like a starving man.

He penetrated her with a pair of fingers, the slick nectar of her arousal easing his way. The overwhelming sensation of his tongue fluttering over her clit and his fingers pumping inside her pussy left Alix shaking like a leaf. She tried to keep her responses in check, refusing to cry out or moan too loudly. She was vaguely aware of the bathroom door bouncing in its frame. Every time it swung back or forth, the music grew louder. A hand-dryer whined in the background. Water splashed into sinks as girls laughed and talked among themselves. So very aware of the close proximity of so many prying eyes and ears, Alix permitted only the quietest of sighs to escape her lips as Mitch drove her to higher and higher levels of pleasure.

His fingers curling inside her, Mitch pegged her G-spot

over and over again. Little bursts of bliss exploded in her lower belly. Those first quickening waves invaded her stomach. She was so close to climaxing. Mitch seemed to sense this and attacked her cunt with his mouth and fingers. Palms flat against the cold metal stall, Alix panted and managed to only let loose a strangled groan as her orgasm slammed her back against the wall. Her hands smacked at the stall and his shoulders. She raked her nails through his buzzed hair and pressed her clit more firmly to his mouth. It was nearly impossible to breathe. Hauling air into her lungs would have made it easier to scream, but she didn't want to share this with the others nearby. This moment, this soul-shattering bliss, was hers alone.

Mitch tongued her relentlessly and only finally stopped when she gripped the top of the stall and lifted her pussy away from his torturous mouth. She silently begged him for mercy as she pulled away from him, one hand on his forehead in a desperate attempt to put some space between her clit and his tongue. Grinning, he chuckled and swiped his slick mouth on her thigh. He scraped his teeth over her tender flesh and bit down playfully. She inhaled sharply but he just smiled impishly up at her. Alix let her left leg fall from his shoulders and then the right. Mitch rose from his crouched position and smashed his lips to hers. The heady musk of her arousal clung to his lips. She loved the taste of herself on him and pulled him even closer in her embrace.

Gripped by the need to show him the same amount of pleasure, Alix started to lower herself to the floor, but Mitch stopped her by gently taking hold of her upper arms. Confused, she frowned up at him. 'Don't you want me to return the favour?'

'Oh, hell yes, baby,' he said enthusiastically. 'But not on this filthy floor. I don't want any part of you touching it.'

Taken aback by his surprising show of gentlemanly behaviour, Alix could only reply, 'Oh.' Most other men would have wanted her on her knees with her lips wrapped around their cock, the state of the floor be damned, but Mitch was more concerned with her needs than his wants. Her estimation of him ratcheted up a few notches. Maybe this one was a keeper.

'Come here,' Mitch whispered and reached for her. He kissed her again, this time leisurely and more sensual. All the frantic need to mate as quickly as possible had vanished. Now it was about enjoyment. His lips skimmed her throat and collarbone. He cupped her backside and kneaded the supple flesh. His fingers traced the cleft there and made her shiver. She bucked against him, wanting more, always more. Mitch's mouth settled on the spot where her neck and shoulder met. He sucked hard, clearly intent on leaving a love bite, and made her head spin.

Alix's hands roamed his body. She slipped them under his damp shirt and enjoyed the outline of his muscled chest. He sported a bit of chest hair, something she'd never found sexy until that moment. Generally, she'd been a fan of the sleek hairless look, but something about Mitch's smattering of crisp hair struck her as deliciously manly. Her fingers glided over the ridges and bumps of scars. He was a few years older than her, definitely old enough to have seen more than two or three tours of duty. She didn't doubt he'd earned those scars in the heat of battle.

Thinking of the awful hell he'd probably experienced, Alix claimed his mouth in a sweet and gentle kiss. No doubt he'd survived some horrible things. Tonight, in this moment, she was determined he would feel only pleasure and happiness. In the great scheme of things, hers was a small and insignificant gesture, but she decided to make it anyway.

As he groaned into her mouth, Alix's fingers tiptoed down his belly and circled his navel. She followed his happy trail to the top of his board shorts. Alix made quick work of the button and zip. His erection sprung free and filled her waiting hand. She stroked the length of his rigid shaft, revelling in the heat and softness of his skin. His jaw clenched as she concentrated her movements along the head of his cock. She squeezed him a little tighter and nipped at his lower lip. One of her hands slipped a little lower and palmed his taut sac. He growled against her mouth as she tormented him with her hands.

She continued to fondle his balls while licking at his neck and using her other hand to pump his cock. Their tongues duelled for supremacy. He fisted her long strands of loose hair in his fingers. She loved the tugging sensation, the slight tingle of pain when he pulled hard and bared her neck. Her hand swirled up and down his shaft. He began to thrust his hips, meeting the downward stroke of her hand.

When he could take it no longer, he shoved aside her hands and reached into the back pocket of his shorts. She couldn't help but smile as he produced a condom from his wallet. It was so terribly clichéd but rather appropriate, all things considered. She backed up against the stall wall as he ripped into the package and applied the latex sheath.

They were both smiling and laughing as he gripped the sides of her thighs and hauled her off the ground. She wrapped her legs around his waist and hooked her ankles at the small of his back. He was so hard he didn't even have to guide himself into place. The fat head of his cock probed her slippery opening, and he sank home with one deep, fast thrust. Alix gasped as he filled her tight passage with his big dick.

He wasted no time in their coupling. With one hand flat against the unyielding green metal of the stall, he plunged in and out of her dripping pussy at a slow but steady pace. Alix roped her arms around his neck and breathed raggedly into his ear as he pumped his hips. His strong legs easily supported her weight. She was suitably impressed by his stamina. All those strenuous Marine workouts really had their perks.

Mitch shifted his hips and changed the angle of his penetration. She clutched at him, loving the new way his cock stroked inside her. Like a well-oiled piston, he slammed into her again and again. With each rough thrust, Alix jolted against the stall. Suddenly, the need for quiet, to shield their actions from those gathered round the sinks and in the adjacent stalls, no longer mattered. All she cared about was chasing her next orgasm and leading Mitch to his. They grunted and groaned and gasped while clasping and clawing at one another.

Alix's clit screamed for attention. The small amount of stimulation she experienced from Mitch's thrusting and circling hips wasn't enough. Her hand slipped between their bodies. Mitch pulled back just enough to give her fingers room to work. Breathing in staccato gasps, Alix strummed her swollen clit. Her belly clenched as she toyed with the pink kernel responsible for her pleasure. Thighs quivering and toes flexed, she hovered on the verge of climax.

Mitch's breathing deepened. Alix sensed he was nearing his release. She flicked her fingers even faster, circling her clit with tight, quick circles. Mitch slammed into her with such force that the stall shook. There was no doubt in Alix's mind that everyone out there knew exactly what was happening. She might have imagined it, but she swore the conversations had lulled. She should have felt shame but she experienced only excitement. The illicit thrill of their public fucking left her trembling with exhilaration.

She held back her impending climax, squeezing her thighs and refusing to breathe, until Mitch was ready to come with her. The building sensations threatened to overwhelm her. Just when she thought she couldn't hold her orgasm in check a moment longer, Mitch buried his face in her neck and took her at a breakneck pace. Alix let fall the walls of the dam holding her orgasm at bay. The waterfall of pleasure rushed over her, the waves crashing down and swamping her in ecstasy.

Mitch hammered through her orgasm. His furious pace seemed impossible to sustain. The friction between their bodies spurred her orgasm on and on and on until she could take no more. The muscles in his neck grew taut. She watched his face contort as pleasure barrelled down on him. Just a few more strokes and he'd be delivered.

Growling, Mitch thrust deep and shuddered. He jerked wildly as he came, his grunts nearly feral. His fingers bit into her flesh as the spasms of his pleasure left him shaking. Her pussy contracted rhythmically as she milked him dry. He groaned against her ear, sending goosebumps shivering down her spine.

Clutched together, they shook from the after-effects of their wild shared orgasm. Alix realised she'd reached up and clutched the top of the stall sometime during her climax.

Mitch placed his big hands over hers and interlaced their fingers. He buried his face in her hair and panted for air. Content to rest against him, Alix remained suspended around his trim waist with her cheek pressed to his shoulder.

Mitch's mouth found hers again in the sweetest and gentlest of kisses. Compared to their wild mating, the kiss seemed almost innocent, but she felt it was the perfect ending to their tryst. His arms trembling, Mitch carefully pulled out of her and slowly lowered her feet to the ground. He cupped her face and caressed her cheek with his thumbs. 'You're so beautiful like this.'

'Like how?'

'With your hair a mess and your cheeks all pink and your lips swollen.'

That surprised her. It seemed there was more to Mitch than met the eye. There was a depth of emotion and gentility to him she hadn't expected. Suddenly she wanted to learn more about this Marine she'd plucked from the crowd for her pleasure.

As Mitch turned away from her, Alix took advantage of his turned back to tidy up a bit and fix her clothes. From the sounds behind her, he was doing the same thing.

'So,' Mitch remarked as she combed her fingers through her mussed hair.

'Yes?'

'I've never done this kind of thing before,' he admitted, looking a bit awkward.

She reached out and touched his arm. 'Me either.'

'Yeah?'

She nodded, not the least bit offended by his surprise. She had been the aggressor in this one. It followed that he'd assume she'd probably done this before with another man.

'I'm not sure what happens next,' Mitch confessed.

Now this question she could answer. 'Well,' Alix said pleasantly, 'I suppose we have two choices.'

'And what would those be?'

'We leave the bathroom and go our separate ways, or you come back to my apartment. We can hit a drive-thru, make small talk …'

'Like dating in reverse?' he playfully enquired.

'Something like that,' Alix said, grinning mischievously. She unlatched the stall door and exited with her head held high. She paused when she realised Mitch hadn't followed her. She arched an eyebrow and held out a hand. 'Coming?'

Smiling, Mitch nodded and placed his hand on hers. 'Again?'

She laughed and squeezed his fingers. 'We'll see.'

Hand in hand, they left the restroom, both uncertain where the night would take them. The morning would bring either the end to a wild night or the beginning of something new and wonderful. Fingers crossed behind her back, Alix hoped it was just the beginning.

A Matter of Taste
Kim Mitchell

I was pretty good at sucking cock. No guy had ever complained. But I never thought I would have to teach another woman how to do it.

It was the fall of my senior year in college and I had just moved into a new two-bedroom apartment. I placed an ad for a roommate. A number of girls came by; the one I settled on was a girl named Kate, a freshman. Kate was a small-town girl, still dating her high-school sweetheart. Her thick blonde hair was long, reaching to the middle of her back, and her slight frame made her appear much younger than her nineteen years.

I attended a number of parties that first month and always invited Kate to come along but she begged off every time, saying that she was going to call her boyfriend. One evening I came home with a hunk of a guy, Mark, and found that Kate was out of the house, and the two of

89

us began to make out on the couch. By the time we had removed half of our clothing I had completely forgotten about my roommate. Mark had taken my top off and had busily massaged and kneaded my breasts through my satin bra and was driving me wild, all the while kissing and licking my neck and the exposed skin around my breasts. I pushed him back and peeled my bra off and then began to unbutton his fly. I kissed his stomach, following the light trail of hair as I pushed his jeans down over his hips. A low moan escaped Mark's lips as my mouth covered his erection through his boxer shorts.

'Did I tell you I like to give head?' I said in a nice sexy voice.

He lifted his hips and tried to jerk his boxer shorts off, but because of our position he couldn't pull it all the way down and the front side of his underwear was held up by his hard-on. I lightly cupped his balls in my hand, enjoying the torture that I was making him endure.

'Do you *like* to get blowjobs, Mark?'

He worked the underwear over the head of his cock and pushed them down his legs. Now his hot flesh was pressed up against my own and I could feel the dampness in my pussy grow even more. I traced my tongue along the underside of his cock, loving the way it twitched under my attentions. I swiped my tongue over the head and tasted the fluid that had oozed out of the slit. I looked him in the eye and ran my tongue over my lips. His eyes were ablaze with lust and he thrust his hips up, trying to bring his cock to my mouth. I scooted back on to the far side of the couch and began to remove his jeans and underwear from his legs. When he was completely naked I once again lay between his outstretched legs and brought my face to within inches of his hard cock. I looked into his eyes, took just the head of him into my mouth and swiped my tongue along the underside, back and forth, slowly. My mouth was watering and a strand of saliva connected the tip of his cock to my lip. I pulled back and allowed him to see it.

All of this playing affected me as well. I lowered my mouth onto his erection, again taking more than half of it into my mouth at once, then slowly pulled back, allowing my lips to drag against his humid flesh. My tongue lashed at the underside of his cock, probing the vein that runs up to the tip. Once my mouth was covering just the tip I slipped my tongue across the head and made circles around the crown. Mark's breathing was coming in gasps and he thrust his hips upwards, trying to make me take his cock back into my mouth. I descended again and, as I pulled his cock deeper into my mouth than I had before, I heard a distinct click. At first I couldn't place the sound and then a new sliver of light grew in the room and I looked up to see that Kate had returned from wherever she had been.

'Oh my – oh, *I'm sorry*,' Kate blurted. Her eyes darted

from Mark's face to mine and then to the cock that was buried between my lips. In the faint light I could tell that she was blushing profusely, deeply embarrassed by catching us in the act. Our eyes locked in a stare for what seemed like a long time and I wondered why Kate wasn't bothering to move. Slowly I pulled my mouth off of Mark's cock and I saw Kate's lips twitch nervously as the head left my mouth, another strand of saliva dripping from my lips.

'It's OK,' I said. My eyes darted to Mark, who had been holding his breath the whole time; his eyes were wide open like he was afraid this would ruin our fun. I looked back to Kate, who was still staring at me, or Mark's cock, I'm not sure. I swirled my tongue around the head of Mark's cock while I watched Kate's expression. I started to take him into my mouth again.

Kate softly said, 'I'll leave you two alone.' She closed and locked the front door then made her way to her bedroom. Mark didn't exhale until he heard her bedroom door shut and then he gasped for air.

'I was wondering if she was going to watch,' Mark said.

I took him deep into my throat and worked my tongue; I massaged his nuts gently as his fingers entwined in my hair and began to push gently upon my head. I backed off and let Mark thrust his cock into my mouth, but never far enough to make me gag. After a few minutes, Mark began to breathe raggedly and I could feel his balls tighten and the vein along the underside of his cock pulse. I pulled back until my lips just covered the crown and ran my tongue along the underside while I jacked his cock with my hand.

As his orgasm exploded into my mouth, I heard Kate's door open for a moment and then close again a second later. I let Mark recover his breath for a time and then he pulled me against his chest. He began to kiss my face and fondle my breasts, but I wasn't really into it any more. I felt as if I needed to make sure Kate was OK.

'How about a raincheck?' I suggested.

Mark dressed and kissed me softly at the door. 'This doesn't mean I'm a jerk just because I didn't return the favour, does it?'

'No, but next time you have to do me twice before I do you.' I smiled and he smiled broadly and leaned in for a kiss before I shut the door.

* * *

I knocked on Kate's door. 'You awake?' There was no answer for a minute. 'Mark's gone, can we talk?'

The door opened slowly. 'I'm really sorry,' she said. 'I didn't mean to interrupt you two.'

'No, it's my fault. We should have been in my room and not out on the couch where you would walk in on us. I never meant to make you feel uncomfortable in your own home.'

She smiled forgivingly and then reached out to hug me. I hugged her back feeling better for having apologised.

* * *

The next couple of weeks were pretty normal; Mark came over a couple of times and we had our fun but always in my bedroom. That first time I made him go down on me until I had come twice, and then we did it doggy-style in my creaky bed. When we came out Kate was in the small kitchenette with a conspiratorial grin on her face. Mark said hello and then left rather quickly.

As soon as he was out the door, Kate began to giggle. 'That's the first time I've ever seen someone just after they had sex. How do you keep from ...'

I looked at her questioningly.

'When you're with Mark, how do you keep from, you know – gagging?'

'What do you mean?' I wanted her to at least say 'blowjob' or something. I wasn't going to have this conversation about sex and not have her use the adult words.

'You know, when you are, uh – kissing his ...' Kate stared down.

'*Cock*,' I said with a slight tone of authority. Kate looked up from her food and directly at me. 'It's called a cock, a dick, a rod. And I wasn't *kissing* it, I was *sucking* it.' I could see the colour rise in her cheeks even more, and deep down the part of me that likes to corrupt the innocent ones was cheering. 'I don't take it into my throat,' I told her.

'Do you like to do that? Suck it, I mean.'

'It can be a very arousing thing to do for a guy. To watch him get that excited all because he wants me to put his cock in my mouth.'

'My boyfriend asked me to do it once,' she said. 'But I didn't have any idea what to do with it so I never did it.'

Kate and I had a long discussion on what to do with a cock after it was in her mouth. I explained the fun in the tease and the immense control over a guy who is that excited.

'I wish I had something to practise on,' she said softly when we were done.

'We'll buy some bananas tomorrow,' I said.

Kate scrunched up her nose and tilted her head and giggled like crazy.

* * *

It was getting close to Thanksgiving break when Kate came to me and announced she was going to try it over the holiday.

'Try what?' I asked, pretending I had no idea.

'*You know!*'

'I have *no idea* what you're talking about,' I said.

'I'm going to give John a ...' Kate left it hanging.

'Say it. *Say* it, or you won't be able to do it.'

'I'm going to give John a blowjob.' Kate's eyes lit up as the words left her mouth. 'I'm going to suck his dick.'

* * *

When I got home, Kate wasn't around so I went about unpacking and then headed off to catch one of my classes. When I got home later, Kate was eating dinner and was genuinely glad to see me.

'Oh, I'm so glad you're here,' she said and hugged me tightly.

'How did it go?'

Kate looked down. 'Horrible.'

'What happened?'

'Well, after Thanksgiving dinner, John and I left my parents' house for a drive,' Kate explained. 'We went out to the lake and began making out in his car. I let him touch me and I was touching him a lot more than I ever had before. I grabbed his cock through his jeans and I told him I had a surprise for him. I undid his trousers and pulled them down around his knees and then I pulled his cock free from his underwear and I tried to do everything you showed me on the banana.'

I was on the edge of my seat.

'Everything was OK at first, but then he just started going soft. I couldn't make it hard any more. Poor John was mortified and after I tried for a long time I admitted that I didn't know what to do.'

Kate's story came out between sobs. I hugged her close to me and patted her head.

'John drove me home in silence and then he didn't call me again until the day I was leaving. I spent the whole weekend in my room crying and feeling like a failure of a girlfriend.'

I clasped her around the shoulders and hugged her. 'There will be another time. Why not invite him up here and try again?'

Kate looked up with grateful eyes. 'You wouldn't mind?'

'Tell him not to spank the monkey before he comes down.' Kate gave me that confused puppy-dog look I had grown so used to. 'Don't worry – he'll know what you mean.'

* * *

When John arrived, Kate seemed really nervous and embarrassed all at once. She knew that I knew she was going to give her boyfriend a blowjob and every time I smiled at her she blushed profusely. We ate dinner and I tried to engage them in conversation but it seemed their

97

minds were somewhere else as the two of them kept exchanging furtive glances. Finally at seven o'clock I said goodnight so that they could go into Kate's room with the idea that I wouldn't be awake to hear them.

I did eventually go to sleep that night around eleven o'clock and if they made any noise I never heard them. In the morning I woke up and made some coffee in the kitchenette. I watched as John slipped out of the bedroom.

After the front door closed, I heard Kate get out of bed and then she padded into the kitchen with her robe on. She didn't look like she got much sleep.

'How'd it go, girl?'

'Not as good as you might have expected,' she said.

'So what happened this time?'

'It was up … and then it was down. It went up and down so many times I lost count. I could get him close and then it was like I didn't know how to –'

'Cross the finish line?'

'I could get him hard. I just couldn't make him come!'

I was surprised to hear her say 'come'. That was the first sex word I'd heard her use without my having to prod her.

'Where did he go?' I asked.

'I don't know, somewhere to "spank his monkey" maybe.'

I burst out laughing.

'Is that *funny*?' Kate looked like she was going to cry.

I pictured John finding a secluded area and jacking off. 'Well, you've got another night,' I said.

Kate didn't seem happy with the prospect. She just nodded her head and took her coffee into her bedroom.

* * *

When I got home the next day, John was sitting on the couch and watching television.

'Kate out?' I asked.

'Yeah, her last final,' he answered.

'Want to talk about it?' I boldly said, like I was a psychiatrist.

'Huh? About what?' he said.

'Last night. What seems to be the problem?'

I slid onto the far side of the couch from him.

He fiddled with his hands in his lap and I decided that he was an OK-looking guy, if a little too skinny for my taste.

'I can't *believe* Kate told you.'

'Who do you think taught her how to give a blowjob?' I was amused when his head snapped up and he looked at me incredulously, his face flushed. I decided to test a theory. 'Don't you *like* it when she sucks your cock?' I asked.

I detected that his breathing had become a little ragged. 'Uh, yeah … it's just that …'

'Hard to take that last plunge?'

'Something like that.'

I went to my bedroom, satisfied that I was right in my assessment of John. I changed my clothes and headed out to some stores to do Christmas shopping. When I returned, the pair had ordered pizza and we sat around eating for a while. I stood up and announced that I was going to bed, adding, 'Kate, can I have a word with you?' Kate joined me in the hallway. 'Tonight, if you try again, try talking dirty to him,' I said.

'Dirty? Like how?'

'Tell him, "I like sucking your big cock," or "I love the taste of your hard prick," those kinds of things.'

She looked at me sceptically. 'You sure?' she asked.

'It can't hurt.' I hugged her goodnight. I walked across the apartment and waved goodnight to John. Before I turned into my room, I gave him a double thumbs-up but he only arched his eyebrows in response.

About an hour after I had left the pair in the bedroom, there was a small knock at my door.

'I need your help,' Kate said. I opened my door to find her standing there, her hair a little dishevelled and her makeup somewhat worse for wear. 'I can't do it. I need your help.'

'John will be cool with this?' I asked.

'I'll *make him* be cool with it,' Kate said and stormed off to her bedroom with me in tow.

I walked into the room behind her.

John's eyes widened. 'What's going on?' he said.

'Her last final,' I said.

John was under the sheet and had his hands over his crotch outside the covers. Kate started to rip the sheet off him when I stopped her.

'Kate, *what* are you going to do?' I used some authority in my voice.

'I'm going to blow him,' she replied softly, her face stoic.

'Don't tell *me*, tell *him*. And don't make it sound like you are washing dishes. This is an act of *love*, desire, *lust*. This is something you *want* to do. Right?'

'Yes,' Kate answered.

'Now, *tell* John what you are going to do.'

'John,' Kate's voice was low, as husky as she could make it, 'I am going to *suck your cock*.'

'What else are you going to do?' I said.

'I am going to *lick your balls*,' Kate said and she traced her finger along his jawline. I looked down and could see his hands fidgeting in his lap. 'I want to make you come with my mouth,' Kate added.

John swallowed hard and looked at Kate as if she were a woman he had never seen but definitely liked. His face was flushed and his hand movements were no longer subtle.

Kate slid her hand across the sheet and pushed his

aside. She began to massage the bulge in the sheets between his legs. John reached out and slid his hand along her back until it cupped her ass cheek. A soft moan escaped Kate's lips and she turned to look at his face, smiling hungrily. Her tongue swiped across her lips as she squeezed his cock.

'Do you want her to suck your cock, John?' I asked.

'Yeah,' he muttered.

'Kiss it through the sheet,' I told Kate.

Kate laid her cheek on the bed next to John's rising cock and pressed her lips against it through the thin layer of material. Her hand slid up his leg and pressed against his balls, pushing them up a little. John moaned softly, his hand sliding lower on Kate's ass until his fingers were lightly touching her panties where they were rather warm.

'Pull the sheet down,' I instructed.

Kate pulled the sheet off John's body. He lifted his legs and laid them down again. She rested her head against John's hip right next to his stiffened cock, breathing hotly upon it. Kate then lifted his cock away from his body and opened her mouth. Her tongue reached out for it and slid across the side, leaving a trail of wetness glistening in the lamplight. With small flicks, she tickled the underside of the head, causing John's cock to twitch in response.

Kate moved forward, positioned her head right over his hard-on and slowly leaned down so that his cock was sliding against her tongue, going into her mouth as far as she dared to allow it. She dragged back, her lips wrapping tightly against the fleshy sword. When she pulled it completely out, a large dollop of saliva dripped from her mouth right onto the head of his cock and slid down to pool in his pubic hair. She pushed her fingers through the wet hair and stroked up his cock, sliding the wetness all along his hardness. She leaned forward and took his cock into her mouth again, her tongue pressing tightly into the underside, and swiped back and forth in a controlled rhythm.

John's fingers dug into Kate's ass cheek, spreading her open and pinching her skin a little. The sensation wasn't painful to Kate but seemed to surprise her. Her eyes widened and she leaned forward more than she had before, taking John's cock just a little deeper. John groaned very loudly, feeling his cock slide even further into Kate's mouth.

Kate lifted her head and began to take John out of her mouth. When just her lips were wrapped around the head, John began to thrust. His cock slipped in and out of her mouth rather quickly and Kate found it was all that she could do to keep the head from popping out of her mouth on his downstroke. She could see John's eyes were shut tightly and she looked to me for reassurance.

'Stroke him with your hand and tell him again what you want him to do.'

She stroked his cock in a counter-rhythm to his thrusting and pulled her mouth off it. Spit and pre-come were mixing to make the stroking very slippery.

'I want you to *come for me*,' Kate said as she kissed and licked his balls. 'I want to make you come. I want to make you come with my mouth.' Kate's voice was filled with need and every time she said 'come' John's body twitched.

Kate looked at me with a raised eyebrow. I made an 'O' with my lips and simulated stroking a cock into it. Kate leaned down and grasped the tip of his cock with her lips and began to stroke him even faster than before. She could feel his cock had grown even harder than she had felt it before and then suddenly he stopped thrusting. Kate looked towards me, worry in her eyes. I made the stroking motion again with my hands and then whipped my tongue back and forth outside of my mouth. Kate's hand kept stroking John and I could see her tongue banging the sides of her mouth as it swiped back and forth over the sensitive spots of his cock. Her eyes grew wide as John emitted a primal growl and his hips bucked one last time. Slowly Kate's hand came to a rest and John's body relaxed.

I hadn't realised how worked up I had become, watching the whole thing. I had been leaning against the wall and when I pushed away from it my legs felt a little weak. I slipped out of the room and made my way to my bedroom where I masturbated furiously before I went to sleep.

* * *

The next day as we were locking up the apartment, Kate was waiting for me as John carried some of our bags to his car.

'So ... what do you do with it after?' Kate asked.

'What did *you* do with it?'

'I just sort of opened my mouth and it all came out and then I got a towel and wiped it up. Is that right?'

'You could have *swallowed* it. But that's a matter of taste.'

She didn't get it right away, but, when she did, we both laughed hard – as hard as a big healthy cock waiting to be sucked!

A Few Hundred Dollars
Emerald

'For example, I could probably save you a few hundred dollars tonight.'

I heard the boldness of the statement as it came out of my mouth, and I almost winced. What had possessed me to let that slip out loud?

For the briefest moment the charming, ultra-collected host of this party in his mansion paused. His smooth face remained impassive, however, and I likely wouldn't have noticed the slip if I hadn't been paying so much attention.

'I beg your pardon?' His tone was polite, drink in midair as he focused on me.

It was certainly not something I had expected to say to Eric Gallagher, whom I'd met approximately five minutes before. Given his position as one of the most prominent investment bankers in the city, I knew who he was, of course, but it wasn't until I turned and found myself

106

standing in front of him near the bar that it became mutual.

He introduced himself, and I told him my name as we shook hands.

'And where are you from, Veronica?'

I smiled. It is my accent much more than my appearance that betrays my non-American heritage, and the question often doesn't come until after I have spoken.

'Venezuela,' I answered.

He nodded. His smooth countenance struck me as predictable given his professional post, and I noticed as well something familiar about it.

'And what do you do?'

'I'm a romance novelist. My publisher, Cat McClean, is responsible for my invitation here tonight.'

'Well, I'm glad to welcome you to my home. One I might have heard of?'

I told him my full name and he raised his eyebrows, conveying, in that unflappable way, that he was impressed.

'Well, it's not my genre, but I have indeed heard the name. Congratulations on your success. Seems you've mastered the intricate art of fulfilling people's fantasies.' His blue eyes sparkled as he winked and lifted his glass.

And that's when it happened.

'Thank you. It is something on which I pride myself.' I looked him up and down, my gaze coming to rest on his as the words slipped from my mouth before I could reel them back in: 'For example, I could probably save you a few hundred dollars tonight.'

Though the comment had been sincerely meant, I was increasingly aware how bold it must sound in polite company. A lump gathered in my throat. I sometimes forgot such things weren't as openly acknowledged as seemed appropriate to me.

Since it was too late to undo it now, I swallowed my discomfort and responded. 'You strike me as the kind of man who has particular tastes and is willing and resourceful enough to pay for them.'

It wasn't an insult. Domination is undoubtedly a skill – some would say an art – and for someone like Eric Gallagher, who cuts to the chase, wants to get exactly what he wants without a lot of fuss and has a whole lot more money than time to spare, finding a professional would be the way to go.

'I see. And how is it you presume to know about my, ah, "tastes"?' The slightest edge of sarcasm blended with the neutrality of his voice.

'Because I used to be one of the ones who was paid for such things.'

His expression changed then, just slightly, and the tension between us – unmistakably sexual in nature – increased. A bolt of heat shot through me as I sensed the moment in which any façade, whether his or mine, was revealed. We stood staring at each other, neither of us moving.

Eric took my arm then, gently, and led me from the room, not speaking as we walked down a darkened hallway in a part of the mansion that was obviously not open to the party. Without turning on any lights, he led me up a flight of stairs, turned right and escorted me through the second open doorway.

The room was in near-darkness. Leaving it that way, he stopped in the middle and turned to me. The outdoor fountain lights glowed through the window, making the shapes around us visible. It was just bright enough that I could see his expression, as I guessed he could see mine.

He crossed his arms. Silence prevailed until his thick voice broke it.

'Do you ever still get paid for it?'

I shook my head. 'It is not my profession any more.'

It had been years, actually – not only since I had been paid for it, but also since I had done it. Pro-domming was something I had for the most part fallen into, and I'd loved doing it with the aim of helping people. It was that purpose I'd held front and centre when I worked. Almost never had I concerned myself with what I liked: in a professional context, it wasn't about me. But that was part of the job, and I recalled fondly my days of being paid well to dominate the myriad beautiful, 'successful', very human men – and sometimes women – like the one in front of me.

Professional domination, though, was often not about sex, and I had found it did not seem common or easy to find men who sought – or at least who disclosed that they sought – what I had provided professionally in a non-professional sexual context. Not that I had tried very hard, but the chance to engage in what I'd done countless times as a pro, in a way that got me off, was not something I had often encountered.

Eric swallowed, and in that simple action I saw the vulnerability just below the surface, yearning and desperate to get out.

There was no longer any doubt that my assessment had been correct. I managed to stay silent and still as my breath deepened. I didn't get paid for it any more, and I didn't need to, but I was well aware that money had nothing to do with what I wanted to do with this man here and now.

To remove professional considerations from the equation and be faced with a man who could easily have been one of my clients back then made the tingling in my pussy graduate to a distinct wetness. The situation presented a compelling opportunity to indulge personally what I had done so many times professionally.

I opened my mouth, but before I could speak Eric was kissing me, his energy, at once aggressive and desperate, sizzling through my body as all questions vanished and the unencumbered understanding of what we were doing emerged like the pearl from an oyster, clear and pristine and complete.

The kiss broke, and I backed away. He looked down at me.

I noticed the chair against the wall – the perfect kind, which I doubted was a coincidence – and pointed to it.

'Bring it to the centre of the room,' I said.

He moved immediately, and my pussy began to pulse in anticipation of what I was going to do. The chair was set on the carpet between us, and even in the shadows I saw Eric's eyes begging for precisely what I was going to give him.

For a split second I was startled to see the habit in me automatically engage. It had been so long since I'd even remembered it, and yet, in this scenario, there it was – like riding a bicycle. The mental restraint, which I'd experienced as keenly as my customers had the physical, arose in my psyche, preparing to erect the habitual barrier between what I did and how I felt.

I shook myself internally and refocused on the man standing in front of me. I didn't speak, and he nodded at a closet behind me near the door.

'Sit.' I barely recognised my own voice. It was not the harsh, commanding tone so well practised in my professional days, nor did I sound the way I was used to hearing myself sound. There was a neutrality in it, but with an intrinsic authority that required no trace of force or effort. As though it wasn't really even coming from me.

I turned and went to the closet. Even in the dark, I found what I was looking for as soon I opened the doors. Carrying bundles of rope, a ball gag and a knife in case of emergency, I walked back to the chair where Eric now sat. I'd grabbed the box of condoms too, and I made sure Eric saw me toss it casually to the floor. I put the knife on the carpet and went to work.

Nothing complicated, no fancy rope work – all I wanted was to hold him in place. I secured his hands together behind the seat of the chair and made quick work of binding his ankles to the front legs. The gag, one of my favourite components, was last.

'Any final words?' I said lightly, waiting for him to shake his head before I slipped the ball gag into place.

I reached behind my neck and unfastened the crystal choker I wore. 'This is going in your right hand,' I told him, stepping behind the chair to drop it into his palm. 'Your safe signal is dropping it on the floor. Got it?' I moved back in front of him, met his eyes and waited until he nodded before I proceeded. It was almost certain he wouldn't have to use it, but it was something I insisted on having.

I stepped forward and straddled his hips. I could smell his aftershave, and I felt a responding tug between my legs. The feeling of his solid body beneath mine made my nipples harden, and I took the liberty of aligning them with Eric's eye-level. I watched him look, and I reached and squeezed my tits over the satin of my dress, grinding

112

hard against the rigid cock under his slacks.

As I moved slowly atop Eric's bound and immobile form, the familiar feeling of power crept like smoke into the darkness, enveloping me until it reached the point of near-euphoria.

A jolt of friction from my clit suddenly made me realise the true power I had. The wall of professionalism I had always experienced as a vague abstraction – perpetual, immovable and virtually unnoticed in the background – collapsed into oblivion in my mind as desire prepared to take over.

My breath was expelled like a shot as arousal ripped through my body like fire. I gyrated hard, my pussy clamouring for attention as I pushed my throbbing clit against Eric's bulk. I felt myself grow wetter at the harshness of his breathing and the intense awareness of his incapacity to speak, to move, to do much of anything but receive and be affected by however what I was doing made him feel.

And I revelled in my newfound attention to how that made me feel.

'Do you like that?' One of my favourite things was asking questions the recipient couldn't answer. I moved my mouth to Eric's ear and whispered, 'I like it. I like it so much I want that hard cock I feel in your trousers deep inside this wet pussy. Would you like that? Would you like to have my tight hot pussy wrapped around your cock?'

Eric breathed heavily, his body twitching as I moved on top of him. I felt his muscles working under me as he reflexively tried to move, to grab me, strip me, fuck me, ram his cock into me and pump furiously, using my wet cunt until he came with the roar of release that was building up in him now.

But that wasn't the scenario we had set up. I lifted myself off of him, his still clothed cock pointing shamelessly towards the ceiling. Leaning in, I ran a finger up the smooth silk of his tie before grasping the knot and loosening it a few inches. I undid the top button of his shirt and stepped back. He would be needing all the air he could get.

I turned, walked a few steps away and stopped with my legs slightly spread. I reached behind me for the zipper of my dress and slid it down. The straps slipped from my shoulders, and the dress fell to my waist.

My breasts, though not yet visible to Eric, were bare now in the dark room. Still facing away from him, I covered them with my hands, squeezing and gyrating as my dress slid to the floor. I stood in a G-string – an article of clothing I'd grown used to and wore not uncommonly now – and appreciated all the more having chosen to put it on tonight.

Eric made a noise in his throat, and I felt myself get wetter. I slid my hands to my hips, turned and watched his eyes fasten on my tits. I walked back and returned to his lap, euphoric in the knowledge that he wanted to reach up and grab me but was powerless to do so. My breathing grew deeper as I ground against him, hearing the whining noise in his throat as I bounced my tits in his face and rubbed my pussy against his hardness, which I could practically feel pulsing against his clothes.

However erotic these actions might be for me in general, it was Eric's inability to move or respond that made the intensity feel like a rocket taking off from my pussy. Removing the threat of interruption has a profound effect on me. My professional history aside, there is a subtle tendency in me to defer. Not attitudinally or ideologically, but simply practically – I tend to withdraw in company and not volunteer information about what I want, or try to influence what others are doing to suit my desires. Generally speaking, I'd rather not make myself noticed and am perfectly content to blend in.

If, for whatever reason, that doesn't happen, then my all-or-nothing tendencies come out: I want to be in charge. This is much more common in small groups or one-on-one, and it was probably why I had discovered I had a knack for domming as well as why I'd enjoyed it so much. The freedom to do whatever I wanted with no interruption or concern about deferring to others was a power play I would admit I unabashedly got off on – sexually or not.

I backed away again and turned around. Bending at the waist, I slid my G-string down to my ankles and rested my fingers against the carpet as I let the light from the window shine on my wet pussy. Eric's breath was harsh, and I didn't doubt his cock was roaring like a trapped, hungry lion with a side of antelope dangling outside its cage. The suspicion made more of the liquid heat I felt on the insides of my thighs surge from my cunt.

I kicked my panties to the side and turned back around. Without speaking, I lowered myself to the smooth carpet, spread my legs and leaned back against the wall. As I met Eric's eyes in the shadows of the room, I reached for the soaked folds between my legs.

His eyes were glued there as I started to play slowly, dancing my fingers over my skin and watching him literally squirm as I withheld my own pleasure for the sake of teasing him. When I couldn't resist any more, I pressed my fingers harder, circling my clit with the singular aim of coming. When I did, I panted heavily, straining not to make any noise as my pussy overflowed, spilling the culmination of my orgasm onto the carpet.

I caught my breath for a moment, then stood and walked back to him. I straddled his thighs but remained standing.

'I'm all messy now,' I murmured close to his ear. 'Sorry about the carpet, by the way.' The look in Eric's eyes said the carpet was not of immediate concern to him. I continued. 'I don't want to touch you now because I'll get your trousers all dirty.'

I looked in his eyes, which were watering with the agony of delayed gratification. Without warning, I

116

reached for his trousers, pulled his fly open and yanked his cock out of his boxers. The very feel of it in my hand made me want it inside me so badly my pussy clenched.

I reached for the box, slid a condom on him without preamble and stood, naked, in front of him. I ran my hands over my breasts and bent forward over his body. 'Would you like me to fuck you?' My voice was low, my nipple brushing his jaw as I leaned close to his ear. His vocal response was muffled by the gag. The tension that flexed and burst forth in his muscles, however, supported my guess at the answer he'd given. I ran my fingers lightly up his sheathed cock, which twitched beneath my touch.

I lowered my body so that my heat rested against the tip of his cock. I could almost feel the desire to ravage me emanating from his body, and the arousal I felt at his helpless position made me whimper. I held myself still, feeling him desperately try to push up into me.

'Do you want to fuck me?' My voice was taunting, coy as my breasts dangled in front of his face. 'Do you want your cock in my wet pussy? Is that what you want?' I said it as though I expected him to reply and almost came at the power of the teasing question that cannot be answered. The cock against my skin felt ready to explode.

I began to ease onto him, and Eric gave a muffled groan. When I finally took him all the way inside me, it was like slipping into the bliss of a hot tub. I closed my eyes and gave my own silent sigh. I paused for a moment before

I rose back up, moving faster as the sensation filled me with a heady satisfaction and the savage desire for more.

A muted cry escaped my lips as I began to bounce uncontrollably on Eric's cock. I slowed, reining in my voice as I sought to regain my composure. It occurred to me that we were so far from the party that the risk of being heard was minimal, but it seemed polite in my position to exercise discretion.

After I caught my breath, I gathered my self-control and stood up. A noise came from Eric's throat, and I felt the corresponding tug in my clit. I could just barely discern the muscles in his upper arms trying reflexively to reach for me as I turned and walked back to the closet.

I was pretty sure what I wanted would be in there, and it was. I palmed the small bottle and walked back to Eric, whose energy I could all but feel grabbing at me as I stood between his legs. I flipped the cap open and upturned the bottle over my open hand.

'Some of this seems nice, don't you think?' I murmured as I reached to spread the lube up and down his sheathed cock. His intake of breath was sharp, and his flesh jumped under my touch as I applied not quite enough pressure to make him come while I smoothed the viscous liquid over him.

When I finished, I flipped the cap shut and tossed the bottle on the floor. 'Are you ready to fuck my ass?' I smiled as I met his eyes, then turned around and backed into position against his throbbing cock.

Eric's breathing was strangled as his hips flexed beneath me. I braced my hands against my thighs, moved slowly, moaning quietly as I eased him inside of me. His breathing became frantic as I increased my pace, my own breath catching as I slid my fingers across my slippery clit.

I sensed Eric about to come, and I slowed again, hearing a groan of frustration in his throat as I gyrated slowly, his cock all the way inside me. I leaned back against his chest, letting my head fall on his shoulder as I ran my hands over my breasts, barely moving as I let his imminent climax subside.

I reached for my clit and stroked it again, gasping as I almost came, finding myself closer than I had even been aware. I ground on Eric's lap, his cock buried in my ass, and climaxed again, biting my lip to keep the scream in my throat from escaping as his muffled whimper sounded in my ear.

Resuming my balance with my hands anchored on my thighs, I began riding slowly, using all my self-control to increase my pace only gradually, denying Eric a tiny bit longer the orgasm that was raging to burst forth – and that I knew would be all the more electrifying for it.

Finally I let go, working to a frenzy as I pounded Eric's cock, my voice escaping in tiny, restrained shrieks. I felt more than heard the roar emerge from him with the come I knew was shooting inside me and the stifled cry that came from his throat. I rode him until I knew it was done, until I felt his body deflate, spent, beneath me, and carefully I lifted off of him and turned around. I caught my breath as I revelled in the last few moments of this dynamic between us.

I didn't get dressed before I untied him, but crouched naked as I undid the black rope around his ankles and released the binding on his wrists. He stayed seated for a moment, stretching his limbs as I located my clothes and dressed in the darkness.

As I stepped into my shoes I felt him behind me. The weight of my forgotten choker pressed gently on my clavicle, and I drew in a quick breath as his fingers worked the clasp at the nape of my neck. I sensed him lower his hands and swallowed as I turned around.

'Thank you.'

He ran his hands down the lapels of his jacket, the polish and confidence back, but with a new touch of groundedness, a centredness I had seen many times but that always displayed itself uniquely. I had been paid for the service of bringing it forth on countless occasions, and it was an endeavour I always appreciated.

Still, I knew this time was different. Much as Eric might have enjoyed it, tonight had been about what I wanted, about the free rein of my own desire that had always been held in check – appropriately – when I was being compensated as a professional.

As I looked in Eric's eyes, I sensed that this shift in

me had altered his experience as well, in ways I wasn't even sure I understood.

'Do you think your guests have missed you?' I continued. I wasn't sure how long we'd been up there. I pictured the elegant, wealth-filled crowd on the floor below us, filled with people who undoubtedly saw my status as an author as the reason I was there tonight. People who would likely never dream that, before I had found success at my craft, I had once made my living as a professional dominatrix.

'Probably.' Eric's voice sounded different. Things had been cleared out; energy was moving differently, more freely, in him now, and to a sensitive ear it was discernible even in the vocal cords.

It made me smile.

'I'll let you get back to them.' I gave a nod and started for the doorway.

'Veronica.' Eric's voice was soft.

I turned back, and he met my gaze from where he stood, unmoving, in the darkness. The light from the fountain shone across the expanse and caught the gleam of his tie, reverted once again to its state of crisp perfection.

'I hope you'll come again.'

I smiled and dropped my eyes to the carpet as I turned back to the door.

I did too.

Suntrapped
Elizabeth Coldwell

Things would have been so different if I'd only knocked on Kelvin's door. When I got no response, I'd have known he wasn't at home, and maybe – just maybe – I'd have taken my textbooks and study notes to the park so I could sunbathe there. But I knew Kelvin's routine inside out, and I assumed that, as he wouldn't have come off shift till six in the morning, he'd still be catching up on his sleep. I didn't want to wake him, so I simply used the spare key he'd passed on to me and let myself in through the back gate.

Kelvin rented the top floor of an unprepossessing little two-storey house on the fringes of a half-built industrial estate. It had antiquated plumbing and a nasty damp patch on the kitchen ceiling that the landlord had never quite got round to looking at, but what made it such a desirable property, at least as far as Kelvin was concerned, was the little area of flat roof that the full-length window in his living room opened on to. South facing, it was an ideal suntrap, and both he and I spent hours basking there whenever the weather permitted. It was where I intended to spend my morning, as I had done so many times since summer had made its first tentative appearance a month or so back.

The roof was reached by way of a winding, black-painted iron staircase. I kicked my sandals off before climbing it, so their pointed heels wouldn't get caught in one of the holes in the elaborate patterned treads. As I'd expected, the blind of the living-room window was firmly down. Kelvin works the overnight shift as a concierge in one of the hotels at the nearby airport – a less than glamorous job but one that pays the bills till something better comes along – and I reckoned he'd be dead to the world till at least mid-afternoon.

Even if he'd been up and around, he wouldn't have paid me the least attention as I shimmied out of my little pink sundress. Kelvin and I have been so close for so long because we know there'll never be any kind of romantic entanglement between us that might ruin our friendship. The reason is simple – he likes boys just as much as I do, though he goes for skinny, sensitive emo types while I prefer my men on the rough and ready side, so I can't see us ever coming to blows over a potential boyfriend.

I know what you're thinking: Kelvin's the stereotypical gay best friend, always there for me when I want to go shopping for shoes or bitch about my day over a Cosmopolitan or two. Nothing could be further from the truth. He's just my oldest, closest friend, who happens to be gay – and very generous about letting me invade his space whenever I fancy a spot of sunbathing.

Still, as I lay back on the beach towel I'd brought with me and smoothed a large dollop of SPF15 along the length of my legs, I couldn't help wishing there was someone around to watch my display. The feel of the sun on my skin acted as a subtle aphrodisiac, warming me to the core and waking the distinct exhibitionistic streak that lurks within me. Maybe I should have gone to the park after all, I thought, opening the psychology textbook I'd brought with me and settling down to read. There, I'd have been able to flaunt myself in front of the odd dog-walker or bunch of lads having a kickabout, letting them admire the way the skimpy bottom of my black bikini clung to my bum cheeks, revealing so much more than it covered.

Though I wouldn't have been able to reach behind myself, as I was doing now, and unfasten my bikini top, slip it over my head and toss it to one side. After all, there were limits to how far you could go in public if you didn't want to get yourself arrested.

But my mind seized on the image, making it hard for me to study. Cognitive behaviour isn't the most exciting subject at the best of times, but now the words were blurring before my eyes, as I imagined myself brazenly stripping out of my clothes in the park, while a crowd of male passers-by offered their encouragement. The lads would stop their football game; the dog-walker would let his hound go snuffling in the bushes. Everyone would watch as I let my top fall to the ground, baring my full, dusky-nippled breasts to their fevered gaze. They wouldn't be content with that, though. They'd demand that I go further, peel down my bikini bottoms to leave me completely naked.

One by one, they'd lose their erections, drawing them out of their flies to present them to me, all demanding that I suck them. The number of hard, straining dicks pressing at my lips, seeking entry, wouldn't faze me in the slightest. There in the strong morning sun I would go down on every single one of them, slurping my tongue over young cocks and old, cut and uncut lengths alike, licking their wrinkled balls and breathing in the secret scent of hot, eager male ...

The urge to slip a finger into my bikini bottoms and diddle my clit was strong, but somehow I managed to hold back. I'd save that till I got home, where I could make myself comfortable on the bed and get down to business with my favourite battery-operated playmate. But I'd got myself so worked up I knew I wouldn't be doing any more studying today. I rested my head on my forearms, closed my eyes and dozed off just at the point in my fantasy where the first of these anonymous cocks began to spurt its load of come all over my upturned cheeks and chin.

I'm not sure how long I slept, but, when I next opened my eyes, it was to see that a looming figure had blocked out the sun. At first, I thought Kelvin had roused himself, seen me on his makeshift sun deck and come out to ask whether I fancied a cup of tea. But as I rubbed a hand across my eyes I realised this person was altogether bigger and bulkier than Kelvin. Alarmed, wondering just how long the stranger might have been watching me, I reached out, seeking my discarded bikini top – and failed to find it.

'Looking for something, darlin'?' a mocking voice asked.

I looked up to see the man had my clothes clutched in his fist, the bikini top dangling by one thin strap, just out of my reach. I almost sat up, in an attempt to grab it from him, then realised exactly how much I'd be showing him of my almost bare body if I did.

'Who are you?' I demanded, trying not to let him see how much his presence discomfited me. 'And what are you doing here?'

'I might ask you the very same thing,' he replied. 'This is private property, you know.'

'It's my friend Kelvin's flat,' I replied defiantly. 'He lets me come up here all the time. Just go inside and ask him.'

'I'd love to, darlin', but Kelvin's in Edinburgh at the moment. I've just come round to fit a new washer in the bathroom tap for him, and what do I find but Sleeping Beauty here, making herself at home like she owns the place.'

Of course Kelvin's in Edinburgh, I thought, huddling into the beach towel. It's his sister's graduation ceremony; he's been talking about nothing else for weeks. Even as I was berating myself for having forgotten his long-planned absence, the rest of the stranger's comment permeated my sleep-fuddled brain.

'Fit a washer ... So you're Kelvin's landlord, then?'

I didn't mean to sound so incredulous, but, from all the discussions we'd had about the man, I'd somehow gained the impression that Kelvin's landlord, Mr McCarthy, was somewhere in late middle age, with thinning hair and a paunch. So it came as something of a surprise to discover McCarthy couldn't have been any older than thirty-five, with a broad, muscular chest and lean hips, displayed to eye-catching advantage in a plain white T-shirt and tight-fitting jeans that had once been black but had faded to something approaching grey, palest and most worn at the knees and the all-too-visible bulge at his crotch. Dark hair bristled on his forearms and peeked from the neck of his T-shirt, and he had the kind of five o'clock shadow on his chin that never seems to disappear completely, no matter how often its owner shaves. The air he gave off was one of nights spent in darkened pool halls and seedy basement bars, and business dealings that weren't entirely legitimate. Everything I'd always hoped to find in a man – if not necessarily under these rather bizarre circumstances.

'Well, now we've cleared up the question of my identity, why don't we get to the bottom of yours?'

'I'm Louise. I'm Kelvin's best friend. If you don't believe me, look at the photos he's got pinned up on the cork board in the kitchen. I must be on half of them.'

McCarthy seemed to consider this for a moment, then nodded. 'Yeah, you do look familiar. Maybe it's the fact you've got your clothes on in those photos that threw me. But then I don't suppose Kelvin's got much interest in seeing you out of them, eh?' He grinned. 'Though it doesn't explain what you're doing up here. How did you get in, in the first place?'

'Oh, I used the back gate. Kelvin gave me his spare key.'

'Did he, indeed?' The look McCarthy gave me made me think he didn't know about any spare key, that Kelvin had decided to get it cut of his own accord. I wondered how much trouble I'd just landed my friend in.

'Look, I know I shouldn't be here if Kelvin's not around, so perhaps it's best if I just leave now.' My natural inclination was to spread my hands in a conciliatory gesture, but I was still lying down, still hiding as much of myself as I could from the landlord's clearly enquiring gaze.

McCarthy shook his head. 'Oh, it's not going to be as simple as that, Louise. I don't think you realise quite how much trouble you're in.' He didn't sound angry with me, though. I'd gained the impression in the last few moments he was very much an opportunist, taking advantage of situations as they presented themselves to him. From the moment he'd come across me, half-naked and fast asleep, he'd no doubt been thinking of what he could do to me, and how far he might be able to push me before he gave my clothes back. It's certainly what I was thinking of at that moment.

'I didn't mean to cause you any problems,' I said. 'And if I'm not supposed to have a key to the property, I'll give it to you.'

'And I bet you'd like your top and dress in return, wouldn't you? Well, you're going to have to earn those back, I'm afraid.'

'What do you mean?' A pulse was beating in my pussy, hard and fast. Being exposed to McCarthy's rough, domineering sexuality and perverse imagination couldn't help but turn me on, making me a willing participant in his kinky little game.

That said, I still hesitated at his next command. 'Stand up, Louise. Let me get a better look at that cute little body of yours.' When I didn't immediately comply with his wishes, he looked at me sternly. He didn't need to say anything more. I got to my feet, using the gaudy beach towel to cover myself.

'Drop it,' he ordered me.

I knew better than to argue. Just like in my earlier fantasy, I was being made to bare myself to a man I didn't know, and, although I could scarcely admit it to myself, it excited me just as much in reality. And it wasn't as if anyone else could see what we were up to; the high walls that made the roof such a perfect little suntrap also shielded it from neighbouring houses. You'd have needed binoculars to get a decent view. Though that image was thrilling in itself: some housebound voyeur getting his kicks by spying on me as I stripped.

I let the towel fall to the floor and stood silently as McCarthy eyed me.

'Very nice,' he said at length. 'You have gorgeous tits, and I love that cute little jewel in your belly button. Very saucy. But that's not really what I want to see, is it?'

I shook my head. I knew exactly what he wanted; I think we both knew that I wouldn't be able to prevent myself giving it to him.

'Take them off, Louise. And don't even think about trying to cover yourself up when you have.' With a jerk of his head, he gestured to my bikini bottoms. For a moment, I was glad I hadn't chosen to wear my white bikini today; at least the black Spandex didn't show the wetness I knew had soaked all the way through the crotch in my excitement. Though that would be immaterial as soon as the garment came off; McCarthy would surely be able to see – and smell – just how shamefully aroused I was.

I shouldn't want this, but I did. Acutely aware of McCarthy's gaze on me, hotter than the June sun, I peeled off the wet, clinging bikini bottoms. When I dropped them to the floor, he lunged down, picked them up and pressed them to his nose. The eager way he snuffled up my scent made me think of a pig rooting out truffles, irresistibly drawn to the aroma.

'Kelvin's been banging on at me for ages to sort out the damp patch round at his place.' He took another long sniff before continuing. 'If I'd known this was what he meant, I'd have been over here a long time ago. Now –' McCarthy waved my clothes in his meaty fist, taunting me with them. I itched to put a hand over my pussy, shielding it from his view. 'I told you if you wanted these back you'd have to earn them, didn't I? Well, here's where you make a start. I want you to suck my cock, and, if you make it into the list of the best blowjobs I've ever had, I just might think about letting you get dressed again.'

His words were designed to demean me, make me think he'd set me a challenge I couldn't possibly complete. After all, how did I know the quality of his past encounters, or how he liked to be licked and teased? And, deny it as I might, part of me wanted to fail, so he'd come up with some even more outrageous request to satisfy him. If he intended to make the most of this unexpected opportunity, then so did I. But my personal pride demanded that, when he walked away, he did so remembering me as one of the best fucks he'd ever had.

Wadding the towel up to cushion my knees from the rough felt, I got down in front of McCarthy. He didn't so much as reach for his fly fastening, obviously intending me to do all the work. Obediently, I unzipped him. It came as no surprise that he didn't bother with underwear, and when I put a hand inside the faded denim I encountered the lurking length of his cock, hot and hefty.

Holding him, feeling him thicken and swell further in my grasp, I couldn't help thinking how beautiful his cock was. Long and smooth, velvet wrapped around steel. Lapping tentatively at its tip, I was rewarded with a little flood of salty juice into my mouth.

One long-ago night, curled up on Kelvin's sofa, seeing a bottle of wine off the premises between the two of us, we'd discussed the subject of what makes the perfect blowjob. That conversation came back to me with perfect clarity, wisdom contained among all the drunken giggling and my awe on learning that Kelvin had sucked off more than double the number of guys I had. He favoured taking as much of it into your throat as you could and simply letting your lover fuck that tight, wet tunnel. I preferred to sheathe my teeth with my lips and concentrate on stimulating the secret spot just below the head. Now, I had to learn the approach that would best please

McCarthy, if I really wanted to give him an experience to remember.

A thought struck me, and I paused in the act of feeding his fleshy crown between my lips. How had this morning taken such a bizarre turn? When I'd climbed the wrought-iron staircase, I'd had no idea I'd find myself naked before a stranger, his cock deep in my mouth. Sometimes, though, all you could do was go with the moment. My nostrils registered the sharp tang of his crotch as I swallowed him, mingled with the last lemony traces of the soap he'd used to wash himself. It was a heady mixture, and I breathed deep, enjoying the primal aroma of sweat and excited man.

'Oh fuck, yes,' he murmured, as my lips inched along his length, tongue lapping eagerly. McCarthy wasn't so big that my mouth was uncomfortably full of him; I could cope with the slight stretching of my jaw, and the feel of his hand gripping my hair tightly at the nape of my neck. When he tried to thrust harder than I was prepared to let him, wrapping my hand around his shaft ensured he went so far in, and no further. Only when I was relaxed enough did I take him deeper into my throat.

Between us, we were acting out an age-old ritual, each of us striving for control, but I knew it was a fight he couldn't win. Not when my tongue swirled over his cockhead in slow, extravagant circles that made him groan and thrust his hips, trying to force just another

133

inch of cock into the soft vice of my throat. I had this big, cocksure man utterly in thrall to the pleasure I was giving him, and the knowledge sent a hot rush of lust sweeping through my core. My mind still played out an imaginary movie where some unseen voyeur wanked himself while watching through his trusty binoculars as I gave McCarthy the blowjob of his life. I slipped a hand beneath my thighs, no longer able to resist the need to stroke my clit. Nothing feels better than having a man come in your mouth at the moment you come yourself, and I'd brought McCarthy to the point where that was inevitable.

Except it seemed he had other ideas. Abruptly, he pulled his dick from the caressing circle of my lips, rocking me back on my haunches. A sticky, candy-pink ring of lip-gloss marked his shaft, visible evidence of how deeply I'd taken him. Almost before I knew what he was doing, he spun me round, easing me none too gently on to all fours.

'The blowjob,' I just about had the presence of mind to ask. 'Didn't you like it?'

'I fucking loved it,' he growled in reply, 'but it just wasn't enough. Unless you like the idea of walking home naked, spread your legs.'

It was a hollow threat, all part of the game we'd been playing since the moment I'd woken and found him standing over me, but it had me moaning and shuffling my

134

knees wider apart all the same. Cock in hand, McCarthy got in position behind me. He pressed the head of his dick to my wet opening. He didn't even need to ask if I was ready. The way I pushed back at him, seeking to draw him inside me, must have told him all he needed to know.

When he shoved home, filling my cunt with a thrust that almost forced the breath from me, I realised I'd found the man of my filthiest fantasies. He fit inside me so perfectly it was as though I'd had him custom-made.

Somewhere in the distance, a pneumatic drill had started up, the constant *whump* of its accompanying generator the perfect counterpoint to our fucking. 'So,' McCarthy grunted between hard, unrelenting strokes, 'are you about to go letting yourself into other people's property again?'

'Depends what the consequences are if I do,' I replied.

McCarthy didn't reply, just chuckled low in his throat and kept on humping his hips in a rhythm that was bringing him right to the edge. I wasn't quite there, and I hoped he wasn't going to leave me high and dry when he did come. He might consider it a perfect punishment, but frustration wasn't part of my plan.

His next words assured me I had nothing to worry about in that regard. 'Touch yourself like you were before,' he ordered me. 'You can't believe what a hot little slut you looked when you did that.'

Only too happy to comply, I pushed a finger back between my legs, rubbing my sensitive bud in time to McCarthy's thrusts. The merest touch had my belly quivering with the onset of orgasm, and I didn't even try to resist its siren call. As McCarthy continued to fuck me, I came with a force that surprised me. Lights danced behind my closed eyelids, and I'd have crumpled to the floor if it hadn't been for him holding me steady.

He pulled his cock free of my pussy's covetous clasp, just in time to direct hot spurts of his come over my arse cheeks, like an obscene brand. He wiped his cock on my towel, zipped himself up again and tossed me my bikini and sundress.

I didn't bother with the bikini, simply pulled on the dress and started gathering up my books.

'Smart girl,' he muttered, catching sight of the title of my psychology textbook as I stuffed it in my bag.

Smart enough to know this had to remain a one-off, I thought, as I prepared to leave. At least as long as Kelvin continued to live here, with McCarthy as his landlord. Anything else would just be too complicated. Maybe we could reassess the situation if he decided to move, for I knew that what I'd lose in a suntrap I'd gain in a hot, dominant lover who was more than capable of giving me all the rough sex I craved.

But that didn't explain why I slipped my illicitly cut key into my bag when I left, instead of handing it over to McCarthy as I really should. Or why I took a last backward glance at him before I began my descent of the staircase, and received in return a look telling me that, however long it took, he'd be waiting for another opportunity to catch me somewhere I shouldn't be.

Having His Cake
Tenille Brown

Jake knew that the average passer-by on 23rd Street's
sidewalk on an average afternoon might believe he was
a bit obsessed about the whole thing.

Even more so, he was sure, if they knew the whole
story.

The truth was, Jake didn't believe he was obsessed
at all. There was absolutely a method to his madness.

Now, keeping himself away, denying himself any
contact at all ... well, Jake knew *that* would have made
him obsessed.

But, no, all Jake did every Wednesday after work was
sit in the same booth inside the same bakery on 23rd. The
same young, pretty auburn-haired woman – her nametag
said Morgan – worked the same shift. She gave the same
sweet smile to the same string of customers and, with
the same polite delivery, always offered Jake a sample or

two of the store's sweets, though she had learned more than a month ago that he would always say no.

Jake had given up sweets, and he had told Morgan as much the first day she had offered.

Of course, she had the curiosity that Jake had grown accustomed to.

Was he on a diet?

No.

A diabetic?

Thankfully, no.

Jake's reason was a little more complex and, after the eighth or ninth query, he explained it to her.

Leigh Ann, his ex, was a baker. She owned her own little shop in the city, and she was always sure to make special treats for Jake at home. The woman could do things with her tongue and confectioner's sugar that you wouldn't believe and Jake explained *that* to Morgan as well. After all, she had to have the whole story.

Morgan didn't seem disgusted by the disclosure of extra information, not even the least bit uncomfortable. That was impressive.

But Morgan was young, it was all over her bubbly little face and tight little body, and Jake hadn't been coming here for that.

He had been with Leigh Ann for six years before she bolted, closed up her shop and sped off to Jersey. She was there baking for some big chain now and was shacking up with some scruffy guy she met at a convention.

Naturally, the whole thing left a bitter taste in Jake's mouth, and turned his stomach against things like cakes and pies.

However, it didn't stop him from thinking about something sweet now and then; Jake was human after all, and he did have desires.

He kept them at bay for the most part, though, and knew for certain that he would have never regained the weakness for it if he hadn't decided on a walk one day and happened upon this bakery seven blocks from his house.

The smell alone was enough to make Jake stagger. Then he wandered inside – just to have a look, of course – and the sight of all those sweets weakened him so much he had to take a seat.

It didn't hurt that there was a lovely young lady – that was Morgan – working behind the counter.

Not that Jake was lacking female attention. There had been the occasional woman in his life after Leigh Ann.

There was Mary, the personal trainer he hired to help rebuild his self-esteem after Leigh Ann scatted. She wouldn't eat any carbs at all.

There was also Nina, the nutritionist who was supposed to help him with the food addiction he was convinced he had. She generally frowned on sweets, though.

Jake was flying solo now and enjoying it for the most part, but he was still a man and he most certainly wasn't blind.

He sat in his booth a minute more. He inhaled the intoxicating scents and his eyes fluttered closed briefly at the smell of German Chocolate.

Jake had very fond memories of German Chocolate, the glossy glaze of it spread over Leigh Ann's private parts, the sticky, sweet taste of it on his tongue as he explored the folds of Leigh Ann's bare cunt.

Yes, Jake knew when it was time to leave. He drummed on the table a few times, rose and walked quickly out the door, leaving the scent of German Chocolate not far behind.

* * *

It had been a long day at the office and Jake knew that it would have been easy to go on home and have a nap instead, but he told himself that he would stop by the bakery for just a minute or two, to read the paper and maybe have a cup of coffee.

The scent of German Chocolate was nowhere to be found today, in fact the smells didn't highlight anything in particular, just an eclectic mix of icings and sweet fruit toppings.

Jake concentrated on the sports section, or at least he

tried to. But two hours later the paper was folded across his lap and his coffee – still untouched – had gone cold.

He was startled by a soft white shirt brushing against his cheek. He opened his eyes and sat rigid in his seat, his breathing now rapid.

'I'm sorry,' he said. 'I must be in your way.'

Morgan shook her head. 'No, no, Jake, I didn't want to wake you. I was just cleaning up.'

He could see the cup of her white satin bra through her shirt, and her small breasts were unbelievably close to his face. She smelled like perfume and treats, and Jake had to resist leaning in for a deeper whiff.

'You're closed,' Jake said, regaining his composure and looking around to see that the bakery was now empty and the street outside was dark.

He was embarrassed now, and fumbling, attempting to stand up and get out of there as fast as he could, but Morgan was shaking her head and holding up her hand to stop him.

'Jake, please stay. I was actually appreciating the company. I don't get it often. I was going to wake you when I was done and ready to lock up,' Morgan said.

Jake steadied his breathing, then he said, 'Oh, OK. I can wait for you, then. It's no problem at all.' He brushed a hand quickly through his hair.

Morgan shrugged. 'Well, I'm done with this table now.'

And there it was again, that smell, foreign yet all too familiar.

'Are you wearing perfume?' Jake asked, though he knew better.

Morgan laughed. 'No, it would kinda defeat the purpose, I guess. I tend to get a lot of sweets on me over the course of the day.' She pulled the collar of her shirt up to her nose and sniffed.

She nodded. 'That's a new toffee icing I made today. Want to taste?' Then she immediately apologised. 'Forget I said that. Sorry, Jake. I guess it's just habit.'

Jake held up his hand and shook his head. 'No, no, it's fine. And you're right, no thanks.'

'Of course,' Morgan said, and moved on to cleaning the next table.

Jake apologised. 'I haven't offended you, Morgan, have I? I mean, turning down your treats all those times?'

Morgan shook her head. 'No, I get it … kind of, but it can bum you out after a while, know what I mean?'

'Yes, I know,' Jake acknowledged.

He didn't want to think about it, though, and analyse it so much that he'd convince himself he was crazier than he already thought he was.

Morgan cocked her head. 'Hey, will you at least have a look, though? The cake is rather gorgeous if I say so myself. You don't even have to stand close to it.'

She pulled Jake gently by the hand when he started to hesitate. 'Come on, Jake, just have a look. It won't kill you just to look.'

Jake followed Morgan across the dining room, behind the counter and through the swinging metal door. He was immediately intoxicated by the many sweet scents that mingled and drifted in the atmosphere.

And Morgan was right. The cake was absolutely lovely. Perched on top of a glass stand, it was creamy and brown, smooth and round.

'Have you tasted it?' Jake asked.

'Of course,' Morgan said. 'I can't send it out there blind. I mean, I'm pretty confident in my skills, but everyone can have a slip now and then. It's awesome, and I'm not just saying that because I made it.'

Then she reached out and swirled some of the icing off the cake and onto her finger. She was standing terribly close to Jake, so close that the slightest bit of cream fell onto his hand.

Morgan grinned. 'Oops.'

She brought his hand to her mouth and licked the icing off, slowly, her tongue doing the work he normally reserved for a napkin or washcloth.

And it was that quick and simple motion that made Jake suddenly nervous. It had taken little or nothing and yet he was turned on, sweating, fumbling, swelling in his shorts.

'Was that OK with you?' Morgan asked, unsure.

Jake answered, maybe a little too quickly, 'Of course. It's good. It's fine.'

Morgan smiled and continued to suck traces of the toffee icing off Jake's index finger next. Her tongue pulsed around the digit, soft and wet. She ended the brief oral session with a kiss on his knuckles.

'So, you're cool, right? We're cool?' She asked. 'Just tell me now if it's not cool and it won't happen again.'

'Oh, it is … cool, I mean,' Jake said.

And he was trying to *sound* cool. He was trying to exude calm because, more than anything, Jake did not want Morgan to stop. Truth be told, he was flattered. Jake was on the other side of forty and Morgan was what? Twenty-five at best?

He had never been the type to go after younger women, but he also knew that there was no time like the present. The opportunity had presented itself, and who was he to turn it down?

And after all, it was *she* who had come on to *him*. And just how did Jake know that Morgan didn't slip something in his coffee, that she didn't set it up just that way so that she could wind up with him back here doing exactly this?

But that was crazy. Jake was crazy.

Sanity intact or not, though, Jake placed his hand on the side of Morgan's face and caressed her soft cheek. He ran his hand over her long, slick brown ponytail and massaged the back of her neck.

As if pulled by some other force, Morgan came closer.

She swiped her finger back across the icing, playfully dabbed some onto Jake's nose and just as quickly kissed it off.

Then she undid his shirt.

She put icing there too, and licked it off. Her tongue on his chest sent tremors through his body. Jake thought fearfully that maybe Morgan might stop there. That she'd think better of what she was doing and quit while she was ahead. And all the while Jake worried and fretted, Morgan's warm tongue travelled the length of his torso. She kissed his body like she was familiar with it, had known it well in some other life.

He felt it coming and suddenly he was afraid she might stop.

Morgan was on her knees now and pulling at the button on Jake's trousers. Jake reached for something to brace himself. His eyes closed, he found the table and knocked a silver bowl from its surface to the floor. There was a clatter, a quick swivel, an echo.

Morgan pulled away. 'I really should lock up,' she said.

Jake, trying to conceal his disappointment, nodded his head in agreement and helped her to her feet. He followed her to the front of the store, where she let them out. Then Morgan walked off in one direction, Jake in the other.

* * *

This time, Jake waited voluntarily.

He knew as well as anyone that chances like these didn't come around often, especially for men his age.

He turned the pages of his magazine like it was no big deal. Like his knee wasn't bouncing frantically beneath the table, waiting for Morgan to be done, wanting Morgan to invite him to the back to view another of her treats.

'Finished,' Morgan called out from the other side of the door. 'Thanks for sticking around.'

'It's really no problem. It's dark out. A lot of crazies walking around.'

'Yeah, I guess.'

Sure, she had only asked him to stay a while as she shut the place down, but he knew a forced coincidence when he saw one.

And then ...

'So, you want to see this strawberry cream pie I threw together this afternoon? I'm trying to get the manager to add it to the menu.'

Here was his chance. It would be even better this time.

'Sure,' Jake said, though he had already begun walking to the swinging metal door.

Morgan didn't hesitate to stick her finger in and bring out a lovely mixture of strawberry, glaze and whipped cream.

She closed her eyes. 'Ummm. Now that's good.'

No accident this time, Morgan used Jake's finger next, dipping it in the cream like a slender spoon, and sucked the remnants off.

Jake let himself wonder if Morgan could be this thorough on his cock, if she could curl her tongue and cause his groin to tighten the way she did when she was gently sucking his finger.

Jake was hard, harder than he had been in the longest time.

And now Morgan was standing closer to him. Jake self-consciously took a step back, his hard-on swelling inside his trousers. He wondered if something would interrupt them again, or, worse, if Morgan would change her mind about it all and simply stop.

But she didn't.

Morgan reached for Jake's trousers, opened them and began working them over his hips. He assisted her with his boxers and then he was standing there, in the cool, dimly lit bakery kitchen, naked from the waist down.

Morgan squatted in front of Jake without a word. She kissed the head of his cock, then took him inside her mouth and ran her tongue along his length. Travelling upwards again, she dragged her tongue quickly back and forth across the rim, causing Jake's heels to rise off the floor.

Now and then Morgan's eyes travelled upwards too, to watch Jake's reaction, and she smiled slyly when satisfaction glowed in his face.

Jake began moving his hips, rocking forward and back, quietly assisting. Their rhythm was soon in sync, Jake coming forward, Morgan meeting him with her lips and tongue.

Jake was afraid of going too fast, seeming too anxious, but, as his strokes quickened, so did Morgan's sucking. She plunged her fingers into his skin, squeezing his ass hard as she began to bring him forward herself and push him back.

She rolled her tongue ring across the length of Jake's cock. Jake gained a new appreciation for jewellery, the way that silver ball felt against his skin. Morgan knew just what to do with it, teasing him, applying pressure here and releasing it there. Jake knew he wouldn't last much longer if she kept it up.

But she did.

Suddenly, Jake's cock seemed to take on a life of its own, moving and bouncing, swelling and throbbing against Morgan's cheeks.

He felt himself coming and felt he ought to pull back, release himself on the floor or on his own thigh, but Morgan held him there inside her warm mouth and took it all in when he came.

Her lips glistened after, seeming fuller, more inviting. She took another fingerful of whipped cream and slid it inside her mouth.

The time it took Jake to gather his bearings, pull up

his shorts and slacks seemed endless; watching Morgan run her tongue across her lips, torture; the walk from the kitchen to the front door then home, long.

* * *

'It's not just a job to me, you know. I really have a passion for it. I know that might seem strange. I mean, it's only cakes and stuff.'

Morgan was naked from the waist up, leaning against the cool steel leg of a table in the bakery's kitchen.

This time she'd shown him red velvet cake with a special cream-cheese icing. It was fifteen minutes since he had come on her neck and chest and now he was sitting beside her on the floor, absentmindedly fondling her tits.

'That's not strange at all,' Jake said, staring at the ceiling.

'At first I thought I wanted to be a doctor or a lady astronaut or something, but that all just seemed so complicated. And I like being creative.'

Jake nodded. He watched as Morgan continued to lick the bowl of icing she had used in frosting the cake. She plunged in one thin, ivory finger and traced it around the edge. She brought her finger up to her lips and pulled the frothy white cream off, her lips protruding, pink, moist and plump.

Morgan looked as if nothing in the world could have tasted sweeter.

Which made Jake begin to wonder just how sweet it was.

'Maybe we should be fucking instead.'

That caught Jake off-guard, interrupting his thoughts, and he looked at her. Was she was bored with him?

Yes, that was it, had to be. He couldn't hold his come long enough to fuck her and satisfy her properly. Morgan was ready to end it after just three weeks. It had been just happenstance, what they had – nothing more.

'Why do you say that?' Jake asked, hopeful.

Morgan patted her stomach. 'I could use the cardio. I'm getting a little fluffy. Don't act like you haven't noticed.'

Jake frowned. 'I haven't noticed a thing. You're fine, I swear.'

She shrugged. 'Still, it couldn't hurt.'

But, as if she hadn't mentioned it at all, as if it had never even been a concern, Morgan climbed over Jake, her head poised perfectly above his middle. His cock rose to meet her lips and she took him in a little at a time, her tongue tracing half moons around his head.

He wished he didn't love it so much. He wished he could be nonchalant about the whole thing and just take it or leave it, but there it was, the same familiar twist and pull in his middle that happened as soon as Morgan's lips touched him, as soon as he felt that sticky sweetness on his cock, as soon as she began that rhythmic sucking.

Jake loved that Morgan enjoyed it, too, that her eyes rolled up and she moaned, that at times her hips swayed from side to side and she clenched her thighs together as if to keep from coming herself.

This time she took him all in and Jake squirmed as the head of his cock repeatedly met the back of Morgan's throat.

With his hand on the back of her head, he held her still as he came, spewing so much hot passion that it dripped a little from the corner of her mouth.

Morgan smiled and wiped it away.

* * *

Jake couldn't say exactly how or why it happened. He supposed it was the fact that the sweet butter cream looked so delectable on the side of her neck. For a while he would debate whether it was her lovely fair skin that taunted him so, or the sticky sweetness of the icing.

But Jake enjoyed both tremendously.

On Morgan's lips, her neck, between her breasts. On her belly, on her knees, between her thighs. In the pretty, soft folds of her pussy, which was shaved bare and which he was seeing up close for the very first time.

The cream and Morgan's own juices were a unique but flavourful mix that Jake consumed hungrily.

They were on top of the steel table – he hoped it

wasn't too cold on her ass – and her legs were thrown over his shoulders. His face was buried in her cunt. His tongue flickered against her clit, pressed gently inside her. He French-kissed the warmth between her legs until she came, shivering and stammering, and, just like that, Jake was hooked.

He decided he wanted Morgan for breakfast, lunch and dinner, would eat icing, sugar or glaze from between her legs whenever she would let him.

But then Morgan fed Jake an entirely different type of dessert. It wasn't as sweet as he'd become accustomed to. In fact, it wasn't sweet at all.

Morgan force-fed it to him, curtly, matter-of-factly. 'So, my last day will be next Friday,' she said calmly, Jake's cheek resting against her thigh. She said the words as if she were tacking them onto a conversation already in progress.

'Your last day?' Jake tried himself to be casual, too, though he was certain it wasn't working.

'At the bakery.'

'Oh, you're going to another shop? Is it here in town?' Jake was trying to sound hopeful, but he hoped he didn't sound foolish instead.

Morgan twisted her lips and shook her head. 'Nah, I'm hanging up my hat, I think.'

Jake paused, careful with his words. 'Well, that seems sudden. I thought this was your ... passion.'

And, for a moment, he wasn't sure what he was referring to any more.

Morgan answered quickly. 'Well, it was my passion, for a while. At least, I thought so. I think I want to check out some dancing jobs. Maybe acting.'

Yes, Morgan was young. Jake had known that all along. She had her whole life ahead of her. She could make snap decisions like that. Pick up and change careers on a whim.

But he'd taken a risk, made a snap decision as if he himself was still in his twenties with the rest of his life ahead of him.

Morgan was talking again. 'We can still see each other, Jake. You can come to my place, or I can come to yours. We don't always have to be in this kitchen.'

Jake nodded, though he knew the truth.

Then he reached over, rubbed the back of Morgan's head, letting her thick auburn hair glide through his fingers. Gently, he urged her south.

Morgan winked and smiled, as if she had been waiting for the green light. She pulled out his cock through the front of his boxers.

Jake held back, though he wanted to be rough with her, wanted to pull her tightly to him and encourage her to suck him hard until her cheeks ached, wanted her to remember for days how it felt the last time she sucked him, when she used her soft, plump lips to coax everything from him and swallow it, take it with her when she left.

It felt as if Jake's cock was wading in shallow water, the way he glided in and out of Morgan's mouth. Her tongue was the guide, leading him in, showing him the way out.

Silently, Jake hoped for patience, hoped to stay the urge to explode inside her mouth, at least for a little while, and prolong these final moments.

And when, a few minutes later, he came and Morgan folded in her lips and smiled, he almost told her, but leaned back instead and squeezed her shoulder, the two of them swallowed by silence.

* * *

He'd stayed away for a considerable period. He had stopped answering Morgan's calls immediately after the last time. He had stayed away from the bakery long enough for them to hire two new girls, to change the sign out front and add three new flavours of cupcakes to the menu.

But there he was again, sitting, wondering, watching.

Jake was better about controlling the urges now, though the girls offered him a taste every time. But every time he said no.

Until one day, Gia, a dark-skinned girl with short

blonde hair, offered him a bit of whipped icing from her finger. Icing she had made herself and hoped to have featured in the shop.

Well, it was then that Jake again, in spite of himself, said, 'Yes.'

Once Bitten Twice Shy
Giselle Renarde

I can't believe the assholes in this city!

Leaving the subway station, I heard this malicious voice shouting, 'Hey, dyke!'

When I turned to confront the bastard, his stupid friends ran away and left him. The guy took a quick step back, but then seemed to reconsider. After all, he couldn't run from a *girl*, could he?

'Come here,' I called, waving the little punk over. He was pretty young, but old enough to be taught a lesson. 'What did you call me?'

Straightening out of his slouch, the guy turned to see his posse watching from down the street. Their gazes seemed to give him strength, like psychic testosterone. 'I called you a dyke, dyke!'

I stood my ground. 'What makes you think you can harass people, huh?'

157

Bystanders accumulated around us, awaiting the impending carnage, but I knew it wouldn't come to blows. It never did. Queer-bashers usually ran off with their tails between their legs once they got a taste of my wrath.

The guy glanced behind him to make sure his posse was still watching, then sneered, 'That's what you get, walking around like you've got a cock between your legs. You want to shave your head, go live on Church Street with the rest of the pussy fags.'

Sheer joy bubbled through my body when he mentioned my hair – or lack thereof.

'Wanna know why I shaved my head?' I bit back. The dude's friends began creeping forward. *Good.* I wanted them to hear this. 'I had hair all the way to my ass until this morning. I donated every last strand to make wigs for kids with cancer.'

His face fell. The penis patrol eased towards him, tugging at his clothes to get him to move on. He was visibly awestruck. I could see his demeanour trying to harden but, like a drunk guy's cock, he just couldn't do it. He obviously had no idea what to say.

'I hope you feel like an asshole.' It felt good to win. 'And I hope you think twice the next time you go queer-bashing on my turf.'

'Whatever,' he muttered, turning away.

'Yeah, *whatever*,' I mimicked, always the – somewhat juvenile – victor.

My blood boiled as I watched the punks traipse down the sidewalk. What mother had raised those kids to be such little jerks? And how could there still be people like them in *my* world? Hadn't we grown beyond that kind of ignorance?

As the crowd dispersed, no doubt disappointed they didn't get their brawl, I ran my hand through my hair. I nearly jumped out of my boots when I realised it had vanished. I wasn't used to the very bare feeling of my buzz cut yet.

As I traced my palm along the prickle of my crown, I heard a new voice, a squeaky girl voice. At first, she just said, 'Wow.'

I turned around, and my pussy throbbed when I caught sight of the pretty little femme. Her long blonde hair tumbled over one shoulder, drawing my attention down to her tiny braless tits. Under a pink silk dress that looked more like lingerie than clothing, her hard nipples stuck out like pencil erasers. She was so lithe, so wispy and feather-like, I couldn't think of a damn thing to say.

'You sure told those bastards.' The girl flicked her hair behind her shoulder. It shone like spun gold in the sunlight. 'That was really cool.'

'Thanks,' I stammered. 'Well, yeah, I think they deserved it.'

'They deserved a punch in the mouth,' the girl said. I couldn't stop staring at her tits. I loved the way they pressed against that pink silk, insistently, like they were speaking to me and I was compelled to listen. 'Just the thought of you kicking those guys' asses turns me on like crazy.'

Oh, God! This little lady was trouble with a capital T. If I didn't get out of there soon, I'd be sunk.

Tearing my gaze from her rising and falling chest, I said, 'Hey, would you look at that? My light turned green. See you around.'

I stepped into the street, nearly getting bowled over by a turning car, but she followed me like a little blonde puppy dog.

'So, where are you going now?' she asked.

'Home,' I said brusquely. I was trying to shake her, but it wasn't working.

'Where do you live?' she asked.

'Not far.' I walked even faster. 'Just down the street.'

How the hell was she keeping up in those spiky high heels? She click-clacked along the sidewalk at break-neck speed. 'What's your name?'

'Basma.'

'Ooh,' she cooed. 'I've never heard that name before.'

'It's Arabic,' I snapped. Why was I encouraging her? It must have been her curious smile. Not to mention those perky tits.

'My name's Lucy.' The girl hopped beside me. 'It's nice to meet you, Basma.'

I turned off the sidewalk and trotted up the front steps of my apartment building, pulling my keys from my pocket. Sure enough, Lucy followed.

Shaking my head, I stood outside my building and asked, 'What the hell do you think you're doing?'

'Coming home with you,' Lucy replied, innocent as anything.

I laughed. I couldn't help it. This was just … insane! 'I don't even know you. Why the hell would I let you into my house?'

'Oh.' Her expression eclipsed. 'I thought maybe, you know, you might want to –'

I knew exactly what she was implying, but shook my head. 'Want to *what*?'

A hopeful grin bled across her lips. 'Invite me up?'

Well, that was an understatement. Hell, I was burning to invite her up to my place. My panties were slick with wanting this little puppy dog who'd followed me home. So what was stopping me?

'Lucy, you're cute and all, but you gotta understand I've been burned before.'

She shrugged, seeming forlorn. 'Yeah, well, who hasn't? I just found out my girl's been screwing around. Life isn't fair. The people you love the most are the ones that hurt you the deepest. So what can you do, right? Fight back? Or find someone else and show her just how bad she hurt you?'

'Oh, I see how it is.' I crossed my arms in front of my burning chest. 'You're using me for a revenge fuck. I was just the first big-ass dyke to cross your path. That's real nice – *real* nice.'

'You said you've been burned.' Lucy was calm and measured, but she got me like a shot. 'So you know what it's like when you just gotta get with someone, like you're gonna die if you don't.'

Hell, yeah, I'd been there before. 'But picking up some stranger off the street isn't gonna solve anything, and I don't want your woman on my doorstep threatening to fuck me up 'cause I stole her girl.'

'You're not stealing me,' Lucy squealed, like a child on the verge of a tantrum. 'Please just take me up, just this once. I'll never try to get in touch after this, and I won't tell my girl it was you. She'll never know, I swear. Please just fuck my brains out!'

A rusted grocery cart squeaked at the bottom of the stairs. When I turned to find Mrs Macintyre watching us, a hot blush consumed my whole body. 'Here, let me help you with that.' I struggled to get myself down the stairs. My legs felt like jelly.

'Oh, Basma! I almost didn't recognise you with all your hair gone,' Mrs Macintyre replied. She latched on to one of my arms, squeezing my bicep while I carried her heavy cart up the stairs. When we got to the front door, I opened it for her, forcing myself not to look back at Lucy. I just wanted to forget about the girl, forget she'd ever stuck to me like gum at the bottom of my shoe.

I helped Mrs Macintyre and her shopping cart into the elevator, but, when the big metal doors closed, all I could think about was Lucy: her pretty little tits in that pink silk dress, her willing smile, her fair skin and golden hair. Was she wearing any panties? I would have laid a bet she wasn't.

My pussy throbbed as I imagined lifting the pink silk and getting a good look at her thighs. They'd be white as snow, no doubt. They'd be so lean I could practically wrap my big hands all the way around. And her pussy! Would it be shaved or trimmed or completely natural? Lucy seemed like the shaving type, but I hoped she had a nice big bush. There was nothing I loved more than spreading open a feathery cloud of pubic hair and finding the pink juice inside, eating it like ripe fruit.

When the elevator dinged, I shook off my fantasy, feeling a little guilty for imagining Lucy naked while an old lady from my building clung to my arm.

'Thank you kindly,' Mrs Macintyre said when I lifted her shopping cart over the raised threshold of her entryway. 'That girl downstairs – is she your new squeeze?'

I bit my lip, trying not to laugh at the older woman's turn of phrase. 'No, she's … she's just a girl I met.'

'Well, if she's throwing you a bone, I say take it.' Mrs Macintyre waved goodbye so sweetly I felt like I'd entered a parallel universe.

I stood in the hallway, dumbstruck, long after she'd closed her door. Did I just dream all that? Had my elderly neighbour really advised me to fuck some girl I barely knew?

Feeling like I'd been granted permission to misbehave, I ran to the elevator and punched the button. What if Lucy had already left? Fuck, she probably had. Why would she wait around after I'd already rejected her? She'd probably gone off in search of some other dyke. God, the elevator was taking for ever. I couldn't wait, so I rushed to the staircase and hurtled down so fast my feet barely touched the floor.

Panting so hard my lungs felt like they were going to explode, I stormed out front ready to chase Lucy down wherever she might have gone. But she hadn't gone anywhere. There she was, sitting on the stairs with her elbows on her knees and her chin on her knuckles. Waiting. For me.

'Sorry,' I said.

She looked up, squinting, shading her eyes against the sun. 'I knew you'd be back.'

'I didn't.' My arms were shaking, my keys jingling in my hand. 'Come up, if you still want to.'

As I unlocked the door, Lucy said, 'I want to.' And

then, leaning against the mirror inside the elevator, 'I want *you*.'

Hell, I couldn't wait any longer. She was oozing sex like a fragrant mirage, her image rippling on my horizon, though she was close enough to touch. I closed in on her, grabbed her, scooping her into my strong arms. Her bright eyes darkened with storm clouds of desire, a transformative invitation. Lucy was mine now, mine for now. Mine.

Clutching her lithe body, I kissed her hard, forcing my tongue past stunned teeth, finding her mouth hot and aromatic like fruit tea. For a moment, she seemed perfectly bewildered, just a startled mannequin of bones and flesh. And then, all at once, she melted into me, her tongue wrestling wetly against mine, her little hands clutching my sides, gripping my fat like she would fall to the floor if I wasn't there to hold.

'Oh, God!' she moaned as I kissed her neck, pressing her tits against my chest. I could feel the hard points of her nipples poking into my breasts as I squeezed her, maybe too hard, because she was gasping for breath when the elevator arrived at my floor.

'Come,' I said, pulling her along the hallway. For some reason, I kept flashing back to that stupid guy on the street, the one who'd called me 'dyke'. Yes, I was, but it wasn't for him to name me. It was my job to assert myself, to name myself dyke, and to show this little blonde just what I was made of.

165

'Get up on the bed,' I instructed, urging her through my apartment. 'Spread your legs.'

Lucy skittered across my bedroom in those cruel spiked heels and jumped on the mattress. I hadn't made my bed that morning, or any morning, and the idea that her bare legs were touching the sheets I'd slept on made me shudder.

Leaning back on her elbows, Lucy asked, 'Is this how you want me?'

That girl's cheeky grin brought out the big bad wolf in me, and I reached back to scratch the nape of my neck. After my brush cut, I was all itchy with sharp little shards of hair, but that was nothing compared to the lower itch, the sweet pulsing throb of my clit.

'Wider,' I said, falling between her legs and pushing them apart, peering rudely between them. I'd been so sure she'd be totally naked underneath that pink silk, but no. She had panties on, the colour of creamy coffee, seamless, made of a stretchy elastic sort of lace. 'I'm gonna eat you so hard.'

'Hope so,' she said, suddenly all cocky. 'I think I deserve it after all the work it took to get invited up here.'

My heart beat faster when she talked that way. I'd always loved bratty girls, though I told myself they were bad for me. If this was a one-time-only thing, it really didn't matter how much of a brat Lucy was. There was something freeing about fucking a girl who was incredibly

166

hot but probably super-annoying and needy in real life. After today, she'd be nothing but a happy memory, the kind I could take to bed with me on those long, cold nights alone.

I flipped her to her belly, tossed her silk dress over her ass and tugged her panties down to her ankles, savouring the sight of those strappy high-heeled shoes. My hands rode her smoothly shaven legs up past her soft, lean thighs. Oh, her ass was unbelievable. I'd never seen such perfect skin – not a pimple, not a spot, just two soaring mounds of white flesh joined by a valley of sweet mysteries.

I wondered if I should warn her first, but decided against it. Surprise attack. I let my palm kiss her ass, sending a clapping noise through the room.

Lucy whipped around, eyes wide. 'What the hell?'

I shrugged, trying to look casual even though I felt weak with arousal. 'You act like a brat, this is what you get.'

'A spanking?' she cried.

I just said, 'Yup,' and I spanked her again.

When my palm struck her little white ass and that thunderclap rang through my bedroom, Lucy balled up my sheets and hugged them to her chest. 'Oww!'

'That hurt?' I smacked her ass again, same spot. Getting pink now.

'Yes,' she whimpered.

'Good.' And I spanked her again, making her cringe.

I loved the way all the muscles in her ass and thighs tightened when my hand touched down. Her voice was strained each time she whimpered little words like 'yes' and 'oh!' In bed, she seemed much smaller than she did standing up.

Her ass stuck out, stuck up, like a cat begging to be petted. I rubbed her cheeks with both hands, feeling the heat of the pink one, the relative coolness of the white one. Pressing them together, I rubbed up against her, wishing I had a flesh-and-blood cock to fuck her with. I could just imagine the straining ache of getting hard and looking down to see a big, thick erection sprouting from the apex of my thighs.

One last spanking, and I flipped her on her back. She was so lightweight it took nothing to turn her.

'You're done spanking me already?' she pouted.

I slapped her thighs, pushing them apart. 'You deserve a good wallop, but I can't resist your little pussy.'

Lucy cooed like a dove, pulling her pink dress up and over her head. Totally naked. White belly, white tits with hard rosy peaks, and her pussy? Oh yes, a full bush darker than the hair on her head, but glinting like gold in the sunlight filtering in through my window. I couldn't get over how beautiful it was, like a blond cloud eclipsing the sun.

'Lick my pussy?' Lucy pleaded, cupping her small

breasts like they were so sensitive she could hardly bear to touch them.

With a little laugh, I said, 'Try and stop me!'

When I pushed Lucy's thighs out, her pussy lips parted and I got my first glimpse at the pink of her. She must have been as aroused as I was, because her little lips dripped with nectar, her clit red and engorged, standing at attention and waiting to get noticed.

'You've got a beautiful pussy.'

Lucy hissed when I leaned between her legs, pressed the tip of my nose to her clit and rocked gently. I could really smell her now – musty, dense, but sweet. Letting my tongue loll between my lips, I licked the base of her slit, nudging her clit side to side. She whimpered like a puppy dog.

'You like it when I lick your slit?' I teased. The answer was obvious.

'Yeah,' she whined, pinching her little tits and arching against my bed. 'Yeah, now lick my clit and fuck me.'

I never felt all that coordinated fingering a girl and licking her at the same time, but there was something about Lucy that made me want to please her. Backing up just enough to watch, I plunged two of my fat-ass fingers into her slit. Her pussy was so slick, so wet, so hot, I slipped up inside her with no trouble at all. She moaned as I extracted my fingers and added another, three now, stretching her tight pussy as she pulled her feet up on the bed. Normally I'd bitch about her getting dirt on my sheets, but those strappy heels were so damn sexy I couldn't bring myself to object.

'Fuck, you look hot,' I told her.

'So do you, fucking me like that.' Lucy perched on her elbows, gazing between her legs as I filled her with fingers.

'Fucking you like this?' I asked, going at her a little harder, a little faster.

'Oh yeah.' Her little pussy milked my fingers, and I wondered how that must feel, that clutching, grasping pressure against a hard cock. If only I could strip off my jeans and rub my aching clit until it grew big enough to fuck her.

'That's good, huh?' I fucked her harder, my path eased by her unfathomable wetness.

'Ohhhh!' Lucy pinched her nipples, squeezing her eyes tight shut and tossing her head to the side.

The scent of her pussy perforated the stagnant air of my apartment while wet squelching noises rang through the room with every pass. My fingers were soaked inside her sucking, slurping slit, and I bent down to offer her what she'd asked for in the first place.

As soon as my tongue met Lucy's clit, she gasped, bucking up against my mouth. I had to slow my fingers because my hand was whacking my chin, so I brought them to a rest deep within her pussy. Stroking her elusive G-spot, I licked her clit fast, up and down, then slowly in large looping circles.

170

'Ohhhhh yeaaaaaah.' Lucy groaned like an animal in pain. She wrapped her legs around my back, digging her sharp heels in, using me as leverage to ram her pussy into my mouth.

Pussy juice ran down my wrist as I rubbed that soft spot within her. She shrieked and hollered, pulling up on her little tits, kicking my back. I just kept licking, going crazy against her hard bud, pressing my thick tongue between her splayed pussy lips and shaking my head side to side. Her wild bush tickled my nose, made me want to sneeze, but I kept at it. Her body kept tensing as she grunted and groaned, and I could feel how close she was. Not long now.

When I sucked her clit between my lips, that was it. She shrieked and rammed her pussy against my mouth like she was fucking it.

'Yeaaaaah,' Lucy cried, still pinching her tits. 'Fuck yeaaaaah! Suck it, suck it, fuck me!'

Raising my chin away from Lucy's slit, I fucked her hard while I sucked her clit. My fingers filled her, zooming in and out, just a blur against her hot pink pussy. The rude squelching sounds competed with Lucy's cries of ecstasy as she rammed my mouth with her clit. Her bud was slippery, pulpy, hard to latch on to, and it kept escaping my lips, making me chase it around, suck it back in.

She screamed and cried, writhing on my bed, tossing and turning the way I did when I was having a rough night. God, the way her thick blonde mane splashed against my sheets turned me on more than I could handle.

'I'm coming so hard!' she squealed, pinching her tits. 'You come too!'

I knew my body. It wouldn't take much to get there.

Letting her clit slip from between my lips, I asked, 'You want me to flick off for you?'

'Yeah, rub your pussy. Come when I come.'

It seemed to me she was already tumbling headlong into that wave, but I couldn't resist her any more than I could resist my own aching clit. Sucking in my gut, I slid the zipper down on my jeans and plunged my hand inside my shorts.

The second my fingers found my aching clit, I was a goner. My legs started shaking and my arms felt numb. I took Lucy's fat red clit between my lips and worked it, sucking hard as I stroked the pulpy wetness between my legs. She'd gotten me so worked up, so turned on that my pussy lips were every bit as engorged as Lucy's. I jerked my head between her thighs like her clit was a cock and I was giving her a blowjob. She really seemed to get off on that, because she screamed and twisted, kicking my back with those evil heels.

'Fuck yeah, suck it!' she squealed, bucking against my face, fucking my mouth.

I still had three fingers lodged in her slit, and I started pumping, hitting my chin with my thumb, too blissful to care. My clit twitched as I rubbed it, whacked it, stroked it beneath my underwear. There was something about getting myself off in the confined space of my jeans that made me feel like a delinquent. And I loved it.

'Yeah, fuck me!' Lucy cried, ramming my face with her pretty pink pussy. 'You're making me come so fucking hard!'

She was making me come hard too, though I wasn't sure she could tell. With my mouth planted against her mound, I was grunting and groaning, but not screaming the way she was. I admired her freedom. Even though I looked like a big bad dyke, especially now that my hair was gone, I'd never put myself out there the way Lucy had today. Once bitten, twice shy, and my poor ego was scarred enough as it was.

My belly buzzed, my clit burning, but it wasn't until Lucy placed both hands on my nearly naked head that my orgasm bowled me over like an ocean wave. I don't know why, but the pressure and warmth of her palms sent me reeling. With her clit wedged between my lips, my fingers plunged deep in her pussy while my other hand blazed against my tender bud. The sheer pleasure burned me end to end, setting my scalp on fire as Lucy rubbed it like a crystal ball.

'No more!' she shrieked, snapping her legs shut and rolling away from my mouth. 'Too much! Oh, God, I'm burning up!'

I knew just what she meant as my clit throbbed against my hand. There comes a point where pleasure teeters into pain, and we'd both reached it, apparently. I pulled my sodden hand from my trousers, climbed up beside her on the bed and wrapped one arm around her protectively, possessively.

Her skin was soft as peaches, hot to the touch, and I traced my fingertips down her thighs, making her shudder and sigh. As she lay beside me in silence, I hoped she would stay that way for ever. I knew the minute she opened her mouth, it would be to tell me she had to leave, go back to her girl and never see me again. And maybe that's what I'd wanted when I first brought her up to my place, but now that I'd devoured her flesh, now that she was lying beside me in my lonely bed, I didn't want her going anywhere.

I hoped the silence would stretch out for ever.